Blindside

PLAYING FOR KEEPS
BOOK FIVE

SAMANTHA BARRETT

This is your warning!

If domestic violence, bullying, drug use, mention of child loss,
stalking, date rape, loss of a loved one and degrading is a
trigger for you then close the book and move on to another
amazing read.
If you are into some dark shit and get off on possessive as
fuck asshole alpha males, turn the page babe and wrap your
heart in a condom because these boys are about to fuck your
feelings, real hard!

Disclaimer

As this is a work of fiction, I just want to say I have tried my best to be as accurate as I can with the adoption process in the US. I have done the research and all I can to make this as correct as possible, please understand this is a fictional book so not everything will be 100% right.

Jaye Pratt Disclaimer

Disclaimer #2
Crue and Saint belong to Jaye Pratt! I licked them and they are
mine.
-Jaye

For my Narne,
You will always be my Narns, my protector from my mum when I
was playing up. I love you Narne, you are one of the strongest
women I know and I'll miss you every fucking day.
Until we meet again my Narne, I love you always.
Blindside is for you Xxx

PROLOGUE

Katie

The night the guys found out she was pregnant

Sitting here on my bed in my dorm room, I look around and hate how bare it is without all of Cody's things in here. Sadness washes over me, how has it been a couple of weeks already since she's been gone? Since starting here at Crestview Heights University, Cody and I met on day one and instantly clicked, we bonded further when we realized we were both on the dance team. The team held a vigil for her but I couldn't find it within myself to go, those bitches on the team never gave a shit about her and the sight of their fake tears would have pushed me to punch them in their fake noses.

I dropped off the team last week as I struggle daily just to get out of bed and go to class. Losing Cody has been fucking hard but being pregnant and not being able to tell the guys out of fear that they will reject our baby, weighs heavily on me as well. The guys think I'm devastated over the loss of my best friend–I am —but hiding a secret this big from them is eating me up inside. I need to tell them but they are both dealing with so much right now. Corvin is a mess and took off to God only knows where. I also know they wouldn't be happy as they have made it clear that they don't want kids. I know they have plans to be drafted and play for the NFL but it's not like I planned for this to happen.

Wrapping my arms around myself, I allow myself to wander down the road of what ifs. Would the guys come around to the idea of us being a family? I know we have never exclusively put a title on what we are but we've never needed to — they are mine and I am theirs. I close my eyes and picture what he or she might look like. I may have only found out a few weeks ago about being pregnant but I already know without a doubt that I'll love this baby. I never thought I would be happy about becoming a mom but since being with Saint and Crue, I've changed my mind. I want a family with them. Before I can fall too far down the rabbit hole of what ifs a knock sounds at my door. A tired sigh escapes me as I climb to my feet and open it.

"There's my girl," Crue calls out as he reaches and lifts me off my feet, crushing me against him. I look over his shoulder to see Saint grinning at us. Crue walks into the room with me still in his arms then places me back on my feet the moment Saint closes the door behind them.

Saint shoves Crue aside then wraps me in a hug and places a kiss on the top of my head. "I missed you, Katie baby." I want to melt into him but guilt gnaws at me. They come over every morning with a muffin and coffee, walk me to class and then come over every night after practice. They are perfect. I just can't find it within myself to tell them about the baby when it would just upset them. I'm a fucking coward. I need to women up and just tell them, but every time I grow the confidence, something always pulls me back. It's only a matter of time before I start showing and I refuse to be that girl who one day strips naked and says 'Surprise, we're having a baby. Want to fuck now?'

"So, what are we ordering in tonight?" Crue asks from his perch on my bed. Saint leads me over to him and I climb up beside Crue as Saint settles down on my other side.

"I vote for Applebee's."

"I wasn't asking what you wanted, dick, Katie baby gets to choose." Saint huffs dramatically while Crue shoots me a wink.

"Applebee's sounds good," I say quietly. I see it in their eyes that they hate they can't fix whatever is wrong with me but neither of them are good at dealing with emotions so they would rather ignore it, brush it under the rug and carry on like normal. I'm a bitch for letting them think that Cody's loss is the reason why I've been acting so weird lately.

Crue places our order while Saint chooses a movie on Netflix for us to watch. This is our nightly routine. We eat and watch movies then they leave. Sometimes they stay but mostly I kick them out because guilt gnaws at me to confess my secret. Our food arrives twenty minutes into the movie. Saint dishes it out, then we all sit here and eat while watching some movie that I'm not even paying attention to.

"Shit." I look over to see Crue has spilled his sauce all over himself.

"I got it," Saint says as he jumps up to grab the towel that I chucked over my trinket box after my shower earlier. He yanks the towel off but at the same time, the box drops to the floor as he chucks it to Crue. My eyes widen in horror. I try to climb off the bed as quickly as I can but it's too late, he sees the two tests with two pink lines staring up at him. I stand here silently as I watch him bend down and grab both the sticks off the ground, saying nothing as he stares at them. Crue slides up beside Saint. The moment he sees the tests he turns pale.

"I... I-uh." I clamp my shut the moment they lift their gazes to me, shock is evident in their eyes but so is betrayal and disbelief.

"Y-you're... pregnant?" I take a shuddering breath and force the words out past the lump in my throat.

"Yes." I watch as their bodies stiffen and their eyes harden, Crue eyes me with contempt, Saint stares at me with accusations clear in his eyes. Fear grips me, I knew they wouldn't react well to the news but I never thought they would look at me like I ruined their lives.

"How the fuck could you have been so stupid?" I reel back, my

mouth drops open in shock.

"You think I planned to get pregnant? Newsflash, Crue, you both were willing participants in the act."

"You fucking did this on purpose to trap us!" Saint shouts, the air rushing out of me. I balk at them, how the hell could they think I would ever do something like this to them. Did I want to have a child? No. Would I have a child to trap them in the hopes they would never leave me? Fuck no.

"Is it even ours?" Crue's question is what tips me over the edge.

"How fucking dare you! After everything we have been through, how can you stand there and accuse me of such a thing?"

"You know we are about to be drafted and getting knocked up to us would set you up for life." Tears trail down my cheeks, they're not tears of sadness but anger—I'm an angry crier and I fucking hate it.

"Fuck you both. I don't need you or your fucking money. I'll raise the baby on my own."

Saint snorts. "You really think someone like you would be a good mother?" Hurt blossoms in my chest at his words. "I mean, you don't even know who your kid's father is, how could you think you would be a good mother? What if it's a girl, would you be okay knowing she's getting nailed every night by two cocks?" I gasp, how could he be so cruel as to say such horrible things about our baby.

"How dare you—"

Crue cuts me off before I can finish speaking. "No, how fucking dare you get knocked up on purpose and then expect us to pay for it. We told you we never wanted kids and even if you do have it, don't expect us to help you. You can't even look after yourself let alone raise a child. Look at the state of you." I look down at my outfit and cringe. I'm wearing stained sweats and one of my old shirts that has a hole in the side. I know I have fallen into a depression since Cody died but I can get better. I'll change and be better.

"I can't fucking believe you would do this after everything that has happened these past couple of months, how could you be so fucking selfish?" Saint shouts. I flinch back a step and keep my gaze

on the ground. I'm a mess, they're right. How could I raise a child when I can barely get my own ass out of bed every day. I'm struggling to pay my bills as it is without the expense of a child. A sob rips out of me as I crumble to my knees and weep for the injustice of this situation. I knew they would be mad but I never thought they would be downright fucking hateful and mean.

"We're done, Katie. You fucked us," Crue shouts. I flinch away from them and watch through my tear filled eyes as they turn their backs and walk out the door, leaving me broken and alone on the floor of my dorm. Screams tear out of me, my chest feels like it's breaking open, my heart shattering inside me. I reach up and place my hand flat against my chest. My heart feels like it's about to burst out of my chest. A sharp cry tears from me when I feel pain in my stomach, I wrap my arms around my midriff as another wave of pain shoots through me.

"Ahh," I cry out and hunch over on all fours. "Oh my God, no, no, no," I choke out as I feel wetness coating my inner thighs. I push back to my hunches and watch in horror as my gray sweats slowly begin to turn red from the blood.

I lost the baby.

Devastation like I have never felt courses through my body. Cries of agony pull from deep within me that I don't even recognize the sounds that are coming from me till my throat grows hoarse. It's too much, I can't take the pain that is ripping me apart from the inside out. They broke my heart and left me, only for a pain twice as harsh and crippling to follow minutes later.

I sit here on the shower floor with the water on scolding hot watching the blood swirl down the drain. I feel Nathan's gaze on me but I ignore it, he came over and found me in a ball on the floor covered in blood. The poor thing thought I was dead. Given recent events I don't blame him for thinking that. He helped me to the bathroom after I managed to choke out that I lost the baby between sobs. Maybe it was for the best, they aren't wrong. I would be a horrible mother, I mean what type of woman brings a child into this world when their best friend was just murdered, their other best friend was date raped and beaten. I don't even know who the father is, I mean we're not even a relationship per se. I'm a fucking worthless piece of shit and I deserve to have lost this sweet little baby.

"You will survive this," he says softly.

I scoff. "I deserve to feel every ounce of this pain. This is my karma for lying and hiding this from them. I brought this upon myself."

"You did no such thing—"

"It's my fault! If I wasn't such a depressed piece of shit maybe this wouldn't have happened." I cry harder now that I admitted that aloud.

"You have every right to feel the way you do. You get to be mad and hide away for as long as you need. Grief doesn't have a time frame and if those two assholes couldn't understand that, then fuck them."

My bottom lip trembles, agony courses through me again as the memory of their cruel words plays on repeat in my mind. Even if I was honest with them from the start, I doubt their reactions would have been any different. I know Saint never wanted kids because of how his father raised him. He's terrified he will end up being like his dad and he doesn't want his kid to feel unloved. Crue, he's too scared to have a child in case he or she judges him for who he chooses to love. It's not like either of them came from a loving family, shit, my own family is fucked up and judgmental. My father thinks I'm still a virgin. If he found out I wasn't, he'd kick my ass out. I will never be like any of them.

It's with that thought that a renewed sense of determination flows through me, I'll no longer allow myself to hide away in my room and grieve alone. Cody wouldn't want that and I owe it to my child to live for the both of us. I'll make my baby proud of me. I'll show them and everyone else that I can be more than a depressed girl stuck in a dark hole, who gets fucked by two guys every other night.

I vow to never allow anyone to make me feel like I do now. I'll never allow anyone the power to break me like they did.

PROLOGUE #2

Katie

The day after she took Alexa to the cabin

Loss…

That one word can affect so many people in different ways. Some will use it and channel it into something useful, others will let it consume them and tear them down until they are nothing but a shell of who they once were.

Me?

I chose to sit in limbo of both those emotions. The moment they turned their backs on me and left me alone to deal with the loss of our child, I shut down. I just lost my best friend a couple of weeks ago and now I'm left alone to grieve the loss of our baby. It's true what they say, you never know what you have until it's gone.

They lulled me into a false sense of security, making me feel safe and loved. I didn't want children, they were never in the cards for me but the moment those two pink lines appeared on the tests, that all changed. I had never wanted something so much in my whole life. The night I lost the baby everything changed, they left me alone and broken on the floor of my dorm room, they killed our baby.

Last night when Nate and I dropped Alexa off at the cabin, so she could go and win her man back, I debated on staying at the motel she booked for us knowing they would come for me but I couldn't do it. I wouldn't allow myself to be fooled by their fake bullshit any longer, instead I choose me and my happiness because I can't achieve those things while they are around me.

I'm not afraid to admit I chose the coward's way out. The things they said to me that night still linger in the back of my mind. How they could have accused me of such a thing is beyond me. I never gave them a single reason to doubt me or ever think that I would do something so despicable as what they accused me of! I thought they knew me better than that but I was so fucking wrong.

"What are you going to do?" Nathan asks me. I stop shoving everything into my suitcase and turn and face him. I feel so bad for dragging him into all of this mess, but even when I gave him an out, he refused to leave me.

"I have to go back to Tennessee. They don't want me here. I need to get away for a while and heal. Being around them is just a reminder of what I lost." It stings to admit that out loud, hating the vulnerability I hear in my own voice. Nathan softens as he closes the space between us and rests his hands on my shoulders.

"Baby girl, those two dumbasses have no idea that they have lost the best thing to ever happen to them." A whoosh of air escapes me. Three days after I began to bleed and thought I had miscarried, Nathan had to rush me to the hospital because I fainted. While we were there I explained I had lost the baby and thought I had fainted from blood loss. After running some tests it turns out, I have a sub-chronic hematoma which means that bleeding is normal and I just need to be monitored throughout the pregnancy.

"I know," I say firmly. "I don't have a choice." Tears cloud my vision but I force them back down, stupid hormones. "I need to get away from here, I just need to go home and regroup."

"Are you sure you can do this?" My shoulders deflate as a whoosh of air escapes me.

"I don't even know if I can go through with the adoption. You need the father to sign the papers to give away their rights, and let's be real, I don't even know which one is the father and neither of them are speaking to me."

'How could someone like you be a good mom when you don't even know who the father of your kid is?' I slam my eyes closed and push their hurtful words from my mind. I know you lash out when you're angry, but their words are the reason why I'm choosing to place my baby up for adoption.

"Fuck them. I'll be your baby daddy." My eyes shoot wide. I pull back from his hold and stare up at him, waiting for the laughter to bubble out of him. It never comes.

"You're serious?" He nods his head firmly.

"Damn fucking straight I am." My bottom lip trembles.

"Nathan, if they ever find out about this and know you helped me–" His eyes darken.

"Let them fucking come for me. They think because I like to suck dick that I can't hold my own. Newsflash, baby, I'd put them both on their asses. If you want to do this, I mean really want to do this, then I'll sign the birth certificate and help you with the adoption."

Nathan has no idea that at this moment he is my saving grace. Without his help, I don't know what I would do. I don't have the money to raise a child. I also know I could never terminate, so adoption was the only option. I was stupid for ever thinking that those two would see a forever type of thing with me. Tears slowly trail down my cheeks as the realization hits me, I'm going to give birth to our baby and never be able to raise it.

Sniffling, I look up at Nathan and force a smile. "No one can ever know about this. We never speak of this to our friends or anyone. They may not want this baby, but if they find out it exists, they are going to come for me. The adoption needs to be closed and I need you to promise me that you will never allow me to hack the system to search for it," I plead. Nathan's eyes soften as he looks down at me.

"You have my word, baby girl. I won't tell a soul. But, I also won't promise to stop you from hacking and finding things out about your baby because no matter what, you will always be the birth mother."

CHAPTER ONE

Katie

Present

I just wish I had known then what a clusterfuck of events awaited me. If I could go back and change it, I would never have placed my baby up for adoption and allowed her to be raised by a fucking monster!

Standing here I just stare at them. Words fail me. Seeing them after all this time with everything they put me through comes rushing back to the surface and pain explodes inside my chest as memories of that night race through my mind on repeat. Their callous hurtful words broke me. The anger in their gazes is what gives me the strength to stand here composed and not break apart in front of them.

Jackson ushers me from the restaurant hastily. I look over my shoulder for one last glimpse of them and my breath hitches. They both stand there stiff, with looks of betrayal plastered across their faces. How they can look at me like that is comical, they are the ones who fucking betrayed me!

I hate that I'm in this mess because of them.

The moment they disappear from sight, I manage to draw in a full breath. A pang of longing hits me right in the chest but I quickly push that shit away. I don't have time to be pining after them when their presence here is enough to fuck everything up.

Jackson unlocks his car and pushes me toward the passenger side whilst he goes to the driver's. Slipping inside, I fasten my seat belt and sit here silently as he starts the car. He puts it in drive and we lurch forward only for him to slam on the breaks at the sight of Alexa, Corvin, Leah and Darius standing mere feet away from us.

"Go!" I snap as I keep my gaze on them—*my* friends. Jackson does as he's told and peels out of the parking lot. It takes more strength than I want to admit to not look back and see if the other two joined them.

"How do you know them?" Jackson asks after a minute. A whoosh of air escapes me as I stare out the window debating on how much I should tell him. Jackson has no idea that I know Crue or Saint. I, on the other hand, know exactly who the fuck he is and what he did to Crue. God, the look of hurt that flashed across Crue's face at the sight of Jackson—nope! I push those thoughts away. They ruined everything and I'm not going to allow them to fuck this up.

"One of their friends is dating my friend," I half lie. I'm not going to disclose to this asshole how much I personally know Saint and Crue.

"Which one?" I keep my face blank and slowly turn back to stare at him. He grips the steering wheel tightly and keeps his gaze ahead, not sparing me a glance.

"How do *you* know them?" I counter. He tries to hide his reaction but I see the way his shoulders bunch and his knuckles begin to turn white as he grips the steering wheel.

"I went to school with them." I fight the snort that wants to break free and look back out the window. Tonight, turned out to be a clusterfuck. This date was supposed to get me closer to Jackson so I could clone his phone and get the passcodes I need to hack into the system, but we didn't even get to order before they showed up and derailed my plans. I sigh as I rest my head against the cool glass and close my eyes. Her tiny little face flashes behind my lids and a pang of longing hits me so hard that I gasp for air. I feel Jackson's gaze on me but I ignore it.

To distract myself, I grab my purse from the floor and grip my phone but that's when I notice I don't have my house keys. Shit. I swipe my phone open and bring up my text thread with Nathan hoping he's home.

> You home? Shit went south so we had to bail, I don't have my keys.

It takes a full minute for him to reply. Seeing his name flash across my screen always brings a smile to my face. He insisted he be able to choose his own name, so I let him.

NATE DADDY

I'm at Lucious, can limp dick drop you here?

I bite my lip to keep from laughing. Lucious is a new club that opened in town a couple of months back and it's the place to be on the weekends around here.

"Hey, I forgot my keys and my roommate is in town, are you able to drop me there, please?" I can tell from the way he pursues his lips that he was hoping the night wasn't over, eww. I'd rather pull razor blades out of my vagina than ever let him touch me.

"Sure thing, Katie baby." I still, my eyes shooting wide and my heart rate begins to double in speed at hearing that name. There are only two people in this world that call me *Katie baby,* and he isn't one of them.

I force myself to remain silent or I risk putting myself and my intentions out there and I can't afford that, not after all the shit I went through to get this date. Out of all the fucking people in the world that I have to suck up to for information, it just had to be Crue's fucking cousin, the person who ousted him and is the reason his family turned their backs on him. I hate this fucking cockroach, but in order to get Adalyn back, I need him and his passcodes.

I thank Jackson for the ride and promise a rain check of our date next week. I feel sick to my stomach the moment he brushes his lips against mine in what I'm sure he thinks is a gentleman's kiss. Honestly, I would have rather him just push me out of the car while it was still moving.

I hop out of the car and watch as he drives away. I give myself a minute to get my shit together before I turn and face the longest line I have ever seen.

> I am not waiting in this line, can you just bring me the keys?

NATE DADDY

> Tell the bouncer you are with me! Us upper-class hoes don't wait in lines, baby girl *eye roll emoji*

I snort out a laugh and shake my head. Seven months ago, I wouldn't have dared skipped ahead of a line but now, I'm a whole new woman and I'm not the bitch you fuck with.

I do as Nathan said and sure enough, the bouncer opens the red rope and allows me entry into the dimly lit club, the bass of the music bringing my body to life. Fuck, I miss dancing. I have to physically push my way through the crowd of people and head toward the back where he said they would be. Women sneer as I push my way past, men try to grope at me, and I bat the handsy bastards away and mentally plot all the ways I'm going to murder my so-called best friend. I begin to think that I'm going to be stuck in this hell until I finally manage to shove the last bunch of college students out of my way and spot Nathan and a group of others in the back corner booth. I wish I could say I sighed with relief at the sight of him but I don't want to lie, I've done enough of that lately.

Nathan spots me once I'm a couple of feet away from him and his friends from school. "You whore!" he screams excitedly. Nathan's *pet names*—-as he calls them—used to bother me but I know he doesn't mean them as insults. "You look fucking ravishing." I wave his compliment off as he engulfs me in a hug and steps to the side so I can wave and say hi to his friends. I've met a few of them before and they seem nice, but these days I'm just not in the mood to socialize. He grips my hand and pulls me after him. We head past the DJ booth into a dark corner where it's surprisingly not as loud. "Spill, now."

"Dinner was a bust."

He pursues his plump lips. "How? You look like a fucking snack in that getup." I look down at my teal strapless mini dress that hugs my body in all the right places. I chose to go with my five-inch heels that tie around my calves, giving the illusion that I have longer legs than I do. My brown hair is loose and flows around my shoulders. I went with smokey eye makeup so my blue eyes pop. I now have a tattoo that starts at the top of my shoulder and goes down my whole arm, ribs, and one side of my ass. Only two people in this whole world would know what this tattoo represents.

"Saint and Crue turned up with the others." Nathan's jaw unhinges, and his green eyes shine with disbelief.

"What the fuck are they doing here?" I drop my gaze to my shoes and sigh. He reaches out, grips my chin, and lifts my gaze back to his. He searches my eyes silently for a moment trying to gauge my reaction. My bestie can read me like a book so it's no surprise to see his features soften. "They saw you?" I nod. "What did they say?"

"Nothing, they both stood there looking at me like they would rather swallow glass than even touch me again." Saying that aloud stings but it's the truth. I know they hate me but the truth is they aren't exactly my favorite people in the world either. They fucking left me! I had no choice, I did what I did because of *them*.

"Well, we can get back to planning and scheming tomorrow but for tonight, you need to let loose and find some good cock to dust out the cobwebs on your stretched-out snatch." I balk at him with my mouth open, the bastard winks and smirks.

"I had a fucking baby a month ago and my vagina is just fine, thank you!" I snap angrily.

"Do you have to cross your legs when you sneeze?" I narrow my eyes at my so-called bestie. Sometimes I wonder why the fuck I love his ass so much.

"No, you wiseass, my pussy snapped back to its original shape just fine," I grit out, and the bastard just laughs. "I want to go. Can I have the keys?"

He stares down at me like I've lost my mind. "Uh, no! Your ass is staying here with me. You need to relax and have some fun." I open my mouth to refuse him but he pushes on. "Katie, you need a break. You have been going nonstop for weeks and you are going to burn out if you don't unwind and let loose."

I reel back and scowl at him. "That motherfucker has my daughter!" I shout. He rushes forward, wraps his arms around me and pulls me to him, holding me close. I try to calm my rapid breathing but it's hard. Every time I think about her being with that cunt I lose it.

"I know he does, baby girl, but you're no good to your daughter if you're burnt out." My shoulders deflate and I melt into him. I know he's right but the thought of spending a night out and having fun while she is stuck with that bastard has guilt gnawing at my insides. "One night, that's it, then we're back into full re-con mode."

One night.

I pull back and smile up at my friend. "Okay." He screams, then proceeds to jump up and down like a crazy child. His excitement is infectious and I can't help but mimic his smile. Slinging an arm around my shoulders, he leads me back to where his friends are. I decide to let loose and give myself one night off to unwind and clear my head, I need this. By the time the fifth round of drinks comes out I'm slightly buzzed and feeling myself. I haven't danced in so long and I'm itching to hit the dance floor. Nathan takes one look at me and whatever he sees on my face has him extending his hand and leading me toward the dance floor. "Nobody's Better" by Suzi ft Fetty Wap sounds out around the crowded club. Nathan grips my waist and spins me around so my back is to his front. I begin to move and let my body flow with the music. Lifting my arms above my head, I wrap them around Nathan's neck and close my eyes as I get lost in the feeling of the beat of the beat of the music.

"Ladies and Gentlemen, we have the New Orleans Saints and Seattle Seahawks in the house," the DJ announces over the music. I tense in Nathan's hold and snap my eyes open at the mention of the two teams Crue and Saint play for. Nathan's grip on my waist tightens as I look up and freeze. Standing a foot away with unreadable looks on their faces is none other than the two guys I ran from seven months ago. The song changes to "2 On" by Tinashe. As we stand here staring at each other, Crue steps forward until he is plastered against my front and my body thrums with awareness at his close proximity.

"This is the part where you fuck off before we make you," he snarls at Nathan. I turn my head to the side to look up at my friend. He looks from me to Crue before focusing back on me. I dart my tongue out to moisten my lips ready to beg him to stay and get me the hell out of here until Crue grips my chin and forces my gaze back to him. His blue eyes burn with anger but I also see the swirls of desire in the depths of those haunting eyes. "Try and leave. I dare you, *Katie baby.*" Hearing my name from his lips has a shudder coursing through my body. Nathan must sense it because in the next second, he untangles my arms from his neck and steps away leaving Crue and I here, alone.

CHAPTER TWO

Saint

My hands are clenched into fists at my sides. Seeing her looking like a wet dream whilst dancing with Nathan has a rage like I've never felt before surging inside me. The fact that bastard thinks he can touch what is mine alerts me to the fact Nathan and I need to have a little *chat*. The moment the DJ announces that our teams are here, I watch as her body goes from relaxed and living freely to tense and on alert. Nathan spots us first, he doesn't seem surprised to see us and that has me wondering if he was the one to message me from the unknown number to tell us that she was here. Crue steps into her saying something I can't hear over the music. After a minute, Nathan steps back and stalks off the dance floor. Crue reaches out and grips her hips pulling her in closer until she is pressed flush against his front.

Indecision wars inside me, do I go to them or stay back here and not allow her to get under my skin again? The moment Crue looks over his shoulder and shoots me a look I know all too well, I know I don't have a choice. They both stand there not moving just looking at each other until I come up beside Crue. She pulls her eyes from him and looks up at me. I hate the way she can still make me breathe easier just by her being near, her mouth parts slightly but no words come. I slowly slip around behind her and grip her just above Crue's hands and press in close so I'm flush against her back.

The song switches to "Taste" by Tyga. Crue meets my gaze and quirks a brow letting me know it's my move next. Before I can make the call, Katie reaches up and wraps one arm around Crue's neck and then uses her other to wrap around mine. Crue snaps his gaze back to her and before he can do anything she has his face pulled down to hers and her lips meshed against his. I watch as all the tension drains from his body. I don't fucking know what it is but seeing him get off turns me on.

I'm not gay! I'm not, I just… I don't know what the fuck to call it but just watching him kiss her has my cock growing hard in my jeans. This only ever happens with him and her. I've never had this type of reaction with any of the other guys before.

She breaks the kiss with him, spins in our holds, reaches up to cup my cheeks and pulls my face to hers. My mind is waring at me to tell her to fuck off, that she will never get to touch me again, but even God knows I have no strength where she is concerned. The moment her lips are on mine, everything else just fades away. Nothing else matters—the anger, betrayal, lies and all of the other shit takes a back seat as I kiss the fuck out of my girl.

Before I can deepen the kiss further, Crue grips a handful of her hair and yanks her head backward so he can claim my spot and kiss her. Fuck, watching his tongue battle with hers has my cock so fucking hard it's almost painful.

Crue pulls back and rests his forehead against hers. "I need to be inside you, baby." Her breath hitches at his words, a part of me expects her to deny us—yes us. If she were to deny Crue then by default she would be denying me.

We made a deal, neither of us gets the girl unless we both do.

"I don't have a car," she says.

I snort. "Let's go," I growl as I grip her hand and drag her after me. I push through the crowd of people. Some try to garner my attention and shout for a picture but I ignore them. I have more important shit I need to do right now, like being balls fucking deep inside the pussy that destroyed my heart and drove a wedge between me and my best fucking friend.

I may hate her for what she did, but right now, I need to feel something other than lost and alone. Since she left, Crue and I have had this divide between us and neither of us wants to admit it is there, but it fucking is! I hate it, I didn't just lose her, I lost him.

I push through the door to the disabled bathroom and yank her in front of me knowing without a doubt Crue followed. The moment I hear the door close and the lock clicks into place I'm proven right. She stands there breathing fast and hard as she looks at each of us, there was never this amount of tension between the three of us before, not even the first time we all fucked.

"Lose the dress," Crue demands. She swallows audibly and I watch as a cloud of uncertainty overshadows her face. I look her over wondering why. We've seen her naked more times than I can count. For fuck's sake, we never allowed her to sleep in our bed with clothes on.

Instead of taking it off, she pushes the top of it down to expose her tits. Fuck, I knew there was no way she could wear a bra in that dress. Fuck, her tits look like they have grown. They're more rounded and full. Gripping the hem of her dress she lifts it to her hips exposing her white lace thong, a groan tearing from me at the sight. She has a tattoo now that covers her arm and her entire side. If I wasn't so turned on, I'd take my time inspecting it. I reach out and slam the toilet seat lid down and step into her loving the way she trembles at my nearness.

"Leg up," I grit out. She does as I command and places her

foot on the lid of the toilet. The way the straps of her heels wrap around her calves has me picturing her hair wrapped around my fist. I drop to my knees and relish in the gasp that pulls from her at the sight of me kneeling. I don't draw this out, I run a finger down the front of her lace-covered pussy.

"Oh, God," she moans as I grip the front of her panties and push them to the side, her pussy glistening with her arousal. Before I can dive in for a taste, Crue comes up behind me, reaches out and swipes a finger through her slick folds, drawing a cry from her before placing that same finger against her lips.

"Taste yourself." Her eyes darken as she looks at him and obeys his command, sucking his digit into her mouth as I swipe my tongue through her folds and feast on her cunt. Fuck, I missed the taste of her. No other pussy can compare, I push my tongue inside her tight, wet hole, loving the way she screams my name.

"Saint." I flick my gaze up and watch Crue claim her lips. She reaches out and runs her hand down the front of his chest. Not even he is immune to her touch, he trembles behind me. Knowing that he is just as fucking aroused as I am, has a moan tumbling from my lips. She cries out and breaks the kiss with him as I suck her clit into my mouth.

"You want to come on his fucking face?" Crue growls.

"Yes," she cries out as I push a finger inside her tight cunt, her pussy walls clamping down on my finger. I can feel her ready to come already which tells me she hasn't orgasmed in a while. Good to know I don't need to murder some fucker for touching what is ours.

"Not tonight, baby," Crue snarls as he slaps a hand down on my shoulder. She whimpers as I pull back and climb to my feet. Her eyes are wide and filled with indignation at the nerve of us to deny her. "Get on your knees, baby, and suck our cocks." Fuck, I hastily free myself from my jeans as she lowers to her knees in front of us. I look over to see Crue already has his cock in his hand. I grip my own and find myself pumping it to the sight of him teasing her. I pause, what the fuck am I doing? To rid myself of those thoughts, I grip Katie's hair and pull her forward, she wraps her sinful lips around my dick and sucks me deep.

I throw my head back and moan, "Fuck yeah, suck it like that, baby." I thrust my hips forward, loving the sound of her gagging around my cock. Hearing that sound and feeling the sensation always filled me with a sick satisfaction that she can't take me all the way. Crue grips her hair and yanks hard enough for her to yelp, but before she can protest, he's shoving his dick down her throat. She grips my length in her hand and pumps me as she sucks him off. Fuck, the sight of her bobbing up and down on him has pre-cum leaking from my tip like a fucking virgin. She releases Crue with a wet pop and her hand replaces her mouth. She uses our dicks to maneuver us so we stand shoulder to shoulder with our raging hard-ons right in her face.

She continues to slide her dainty little hands up and down our lengths, just the way she knows we like it. That's the thing about fucking an ex, the sex is always fire because you know what each other likes, but the hurt and pain still festers just beneath the surface, that rage spills over into it and tricks your brain into forgetting, even just momentarily. She pulls us closer together, our tips touching ever so slightly with each pump of her hand, Crue thrusts forward and when his head touches mine it sends shivers down my spine. The moment she tries to take us both in her mouth at once has Crue moaning in pleasure and I just stand here stunned.

Our cocks are touching and all I can hear is my father's voice in my head. Closing my eyes, I ball my hands into fists and breath. I should be appalled, or raging but I'm... not. Before I get too lost in the thought, I pull myself free and haul her to her feet, clasp her face between my hands and kiss her, loving the taste of *us* on her tongue.

"Fuck her," Crue demands and has us breaking apart, both looking at him. "Bend her ass over that basin and sink with your dick so deep inside her she creams all over you. I want her to watch as she screams for you."

Katie does as he says and bends over gripping the basin. I have other ideas though. I grip her thong and pull it down her legs, shoving it in my pocket. Gripping the globes of her ass I part her cheeks and spit before I begin to eat her from behind. It's been too fucking long since I've tasted her like this. If we had lube, we'd both be fucking her right now.

"Fuck yes, Saint, eat it like that, baby." She knows better than to give orders, I draw back and land a swift slap across her backside, loving the sound of the scream that rips from her lips. I gather her hair and grip it in one hand as I use the other to line my cock up with her cunt. A good man would slide in slowly but I've never claimed to be good at anything other than football. I slam inside her again, relishing in the strangled cries of pleasure that rip from her. I see tears cloud her vision in the mirror, and my anger takes hold. I fuck her ruthlessly, I don't even care if she comes or not, this is about me, not her. She left, she needs to feel the pain I did waking up without her every day, not knowing if she was alive or dead. "Oh fuck," she yells so fucking loud, I think everyone in the club will hear.

"You gonna take my cum like the dirty fucking girl you are?" I growl.

"Fuck yes, give it to me." Jesus, as if her words have a direct line to my cock my balls begin to tighten and then I'm coming. I hold her gaze in the mirror as we both come apart, together. This begins to feel too intimate, so I pull out and step back as Crue steps up behind her and shoves a finger inside her tight wet cunt drawing another cry from her. He pulls that finger out and I expect him to hold it out to her to suck it clean but I'm stunned silent when he sucks his own finger between his lips, moaning. My lusted gaze never leaves his mouth, enthralled that my best friend is tasting my cum.

"Fuck, you both taste so good together," he growls approvingly. Crue isn't gentle with her either, he lines himself up with her entrance and slams inside her tight pussy. They both cry out and I stand there and really watch them both for the first time and my heart thumps wildly in my chest. Fuck feelings. My dick doesn't get the memo that it's rest time, it's hard again within minutes. My palm wraps around my rock-hard length, my eyes zero in on the juices running down her thighs between them, her soft mewls get louder and I cum the moment he bottoms out inside her.

CHAPTER THREE

Fuck!

Holy shit, it's been so long since I've had them both and oh my God, they feel fucking amazing inside me. I feel complete again. Crue grips my waist in a punishing hold that I know will bruise but I don't have it in me to give a damn. I want to wear the brand of their love, their ownership, it will be the only way I'll know this wasn't just a dream.

"Fuck yes, take my cock," Crue grits out as he slams inside me again. I push back against him, needing more. He pulls free, turns me around, grips my waist and lifts me so I'm balancing on the edge of the sink. "Wrap your arms around me." I do as he says and the moment he slides back inside my greedy cunt, I lock my legs around his waist and cry out, fuck he feels so deep. Saint slides up beside us, grips my chin and pulls my face to him. His gaze bores into me, it feels like those pale green eyes can see right past my walls and into my soul.

He smashes his lips against mine, swallowing my cry as Crue hits that wonderful G spot. He continues to fuck me senseless as Saint fucks my mouth with his tongue. Fuck, on their own these two are lethal but together they are a fucking force of mass destruction.

Saint breaks our kiss but keeps my chin in his hold as he stares directly into my eyes. "You like how he fucks you, *Katie baby*?" Hearing my nickname from Crue had me feeling hot and needy, but hearing it from Saint has a sense of dread settling over me, he didn't say it with love or longing. "Answer me."

"Yes," I cry out as Crue slams into me again and again, he leans down and captures my nipple in his mouth and that's when I come so fucking hard I see stars, Crue roars out his own release coming deep inside my pussy. The moment he releases my nipple to try and catch his breath, horror fills me at the sight of my milk spraying out and landing on his shirt.

Saint and Crue both stare at it with mortified looks on their faces, fuck!

I bat Saint's hand away and shove Crue back a step before climbing to my feet, neither of them says a word and I'm grateful for that. The moment I sort my dress, I race from the bathroom ignoring them calling after me. How could I have been so fucking stupid. I head straight for the exit and by the grace of God Nathan is standing there talking to some guy. His gaze cuts to me and one look at my disheveled appearance is all it takes for him to break away from the guy, then he is ushering me out of the club.

"So, your pussy isn't a squirter but your titties are?" I groan and smack my head against the counter. Nathan laughs at my expense. I mean, what the hell did I expect? Confiding in Nathan is like confiding in a toddler, the guy makes a joke out of everything.

"I want to die. That was fucking humiliating!" I grumble as I lift my head to glare at my friend, his eyes soften.

"Look, they're guys. They are gonna have no idea what the fuck happened so don't panic. We need to forget about them and work out what the hell we are going to do about Jackson. We need to lay low until tomorrow. Ben was saying the teams are heading back today so let's not tempt fate and go into town today and risk seeing your boys."

Hearing that they are leaving has a pang of sadness hitting me in the chest. I shove that feeling away. If it's a choice between them or her, I choose her. I'll always choose her over everyone. I made a stupid decision thinking she would have a better life without me and her fathers that didn't want her, but I was fucking wrong. Now I'll do whatever the fuck I have to so I can get my little girl away from that monster.

"How did they even know we were there? I mean, they were at dinner with the others and then out of nowhere they show up at Lucious?" Nathan's eyes dart around the room refusing to look at me. My jaw unhinges. "You told them!" I accuse and he pins me with a pleading look, urging me to understand.

"You needed that closure—"

I throw my hands up in the air. "Don't you get it!" I shout. "There is no closure from them. Even after them walking out on me when they found out I was pregnant and leaving me to deal with what I thought was a miscarriage alone, I still pined for them. I'm still fucking in love with them, Nate, and I hate it." A lump forms in my throat. Nathan rushes over to me and pulls me in for a hug.

"I'm so sorry, baby girl. I thought I was helping." I melt into him.

"It's not your fault. Them being around just puts all my plans at risk. He already knows I'm onto him and if he found out Saint and Crue were helping me, he would disappear and I wouldn't be able to get my little girl back." As good as I am at hacking, he is better at covering his tracks and my only way to find my little girl is through Jackson. Even that bastard is good at hiding his files and passcodes behind encrypted firewalls that I can't access remotely.

"I know. I'm sorry, I'll never meddle in your business with them again." I mumble my thanks into his chest. "Also, while Alexa, Leah and Val are in town did you want to… maybe see them?" I pull back and stare up at him, as much as I want to say yes I know the girls will push me for answers and right now, I can't give them any. Tears cloud my vision as I shake my head. Nate sighs and nods. I feel guilty that he feels like he can't go and see them out of some sort of misplaced loyalty to me.

"You go, I know you miss them—"

He cuts in before I can finish. "No. I don't want to lie to them either. Once this is all over then I can go to them and catch up."

"Nate, even when this is over I… I don't know if they will welcome me back." His features harden.

"You listen to me, you did nothing wrong and if those twits want to say otherwise, they can come to me because I have a few fucking things I need to get off my chest where those two dumb fucks are concerned." The malice in his tone has me standing straight and pulling back to stare up at my friend. I'm looking at him in a whole new light now and I can't say I'm mad about it.

Monday rolls around and the town is back to being quiet and empty, the hype of the Seahawks and Saints being here is wearing off as well as the New Year. Unlike Nathan, who went out and celebrated the New Year, I chose to stay in and wallow in my own self-pity, I'll celebrate that holiday when I end this shit.

As I pass by Lucious, a shiver runs down my spine as memories of how they made me come so many times plays through my mind. Don't get me wrong, I wasn't a virgin when I met the guys and I had orgasmed before whilst having sex, but those times were nothing compared to how they made my body sing and move to the beat they create.

My phone rings, pulling me from my thoughts. I check the number to see it's the PI Troy had used to track down Val's stalker. Paying this guy cost me half my paycheck, the other half goes toward covering rent and all that shit. I answer the call through the car's Bluetooth system.

"Hey, did you manage to get a location?" I ask.

"No. The address where the last email came from is a dud, it's a construction site."

Fuck, that was my last lead.

"Okay, that was all I had. Give me a couple days, I have another angle to work and let's just hope it pans out." I say before disconnecting the call, I pull into the staff lot behind the lingerie store I work at. Don't judge me, it was the only place hiring at the time plus, the owner allows me to study while I work so it's perfect. I can't go to college full time, I don't have the money and my parents cut me off when I came home pregnant and unwed. They are your typical old school, southern family. It was easier for them to cut me off and act like I don't exist then face the shame of what their friends would think of their pregnant nineteen-year-old daughter. Imagine if they found out I was fucking two guys and had no idea which one the father was. Oh, the travesty. I can picture my mother clutching her fake pearls and fainting the moment she found out.

Heading inside I stash my bag and laptop behind the counter as I go about my morning routine and open up the shop. Mondays and Tuesdays are normally our quiet days so I get most of my study and school work done then. I'm an online student and don't have the luxury now of attending classes in person, it sucked at the start but over time I've grown used to it. I made a choice to have a baby and I don't regret it. Once everything is open I hop behind the counter and set up my laptop, I bring up my browser and immediately tense. Right there on the front page of the news is a picture of me, Saint and Crue together on the dance floor with the headline, *who is the mystery girl in the NFL sandwich?* Fuck. I set out to have the article pulled down and check all the other news outlets making sure they aren't covering the story as well. Any article that mentions the guys I shut down, I even keep an eye on BCD'S and make sure their company or the others don't make a bad headline.

I may have chosen to leave them behind but that doesn't mean I don't care about all of them. The bell above the door jingles alerting me that someone has come in, I finish up and close the lid of my laptop, plastering a smile on my face as I look up and say.

"Welcome to——" The words die in my throat at the sight of Corvin, Alexa, Darius and Leah. I look each of them over and note they all look good, happy even. I heard that Beck and Val tied the knot and Corvin proposed to Alexa at Christmas.

"Working on New Year's Day, how Katie of you," Corvin snarks. I allow it to roll off my shoulders and choose not to dwell on the bitterness in his tone. I know my leaving didn't just hurt the two guys, it hurt the others as well.

"Nathan told you where I was?" I breathe out. The moment Leah frowns and cocks her head to the side, I know I just fucked up.

"Nathan is here? With you?" I cringe.

"Yeah, Leah, he's here," I answer. A look of hurt flashes across her face before she quickly masks it. I hate hurting her. Leah is one of my best friends and I know me leaving without a word must have hurt her badly. "What are you all doing here?"

Alexa breaks away from the others and comes to stand on the other side of the counter, her gaze is sharp and accusing as she stares me down. "You once told me to stop trying to find every excuse I could to not be with Corvin. How about you take your own advice." I grit my teeth and white knuckle the edge of the counter.

"You have no idea what the fuck happened," I seethe. Corvin steps forward drawing my attention to him, he halts his movements the moment he sees the look on my face. "You all come in here ready to go to bat for Crue and Saint and yet none of you know what happened—"

"They feel fucking horrible for leaving you to deal with the loss of the—" I cut Alexa off before she can finish.

"Stop!" She clamps her mouth closed, and Leah steps forward wearing a look of guilt as she looks me over.

"We saw you driving through the main street and followed you, we thought you might be happy to see us but I guess... we were wrong." My shoulders deflate as guilt swims inside me. "We're in town for one more night, if you want to catch up before we leave tomorrow, that would be amazing."

Before I can stop myself, the words spew out of me. "I'd love to." Leah beams at me and rattles off the time and place to meet them tonight. I promise to bring Nathan along with me. As they leave, I find myself smiling at the thought of being able to hang out with my friends again. I know Darius and Corvin are pissed at me but if they knew the truth, they'd both be rethinking their attitude toward me.

CHAPTER FOUR

"Why the fuck are we doing a stupid dinner?" Saint moans from behind me. I turn to see him sprawled out across my bed. He looks good in low-slung dark-wash jeans, black boots and a plain white shirt that stretches across his chest perfectly. His hair is a tousled mess. I cock my head to the side and just take him in. It's no secret that I have feelings for him, everyone knows it except Saint. I've never admitted that shit to him in case I ruined what we have. Truth is, since Katie left, we have had this… divide between us and I don't know how to close that gap.

"Because we fly out tomorrow and won't see the family for a few months." He lulls his head to the side and pins me with a *duh* look.

"I'd rather stay here and cuddle up to you while we watch rom coms and make out." I snort and brush off his comment like it didn't just have my cock twitching my pants. He's always joked about shit like this and I've gone along with it every time until recently. It's no longer a joke to me. What he says is what I want and I can't keep downplaying that shit anymore.

"Yeah well, we can't always get what we want now, can

we?" His face contorts into one of confusion. Before he can question me on my outburst, I grab my Seahawk Letterman jacket off the back of the chair and head for the door. "You coming?" I call over my shoulder.

"I wish," I hear him mumble behind me. I know it's not his fault. Saint has always been blind to my advances toward him. Seeing him fuck his way through the population of girls at CHU killed me. It wasn't until we met Katie that shit changed. Don't get me wrong, I'm still in love with Saint but Katie managed to weasel her way inside my heart without much effort. She is the person that brought us closer without even meaning to.

At the start, I went along with fucking her just to feel closer to Saint but over time it stopped being just about him and shifted to it becoming about the three of us and the life we could build together. Yes, Katie has fucked both of us at the same time but Saint and I have never crossed that line, not because of me but because I don't want to push him only to find out he doesn't feel the same way about me.

The drive to the restaurant is filled with tension. Rather than sit in awkward silence, I play the radio loudly. I pull up out front of the restaurant and scrunch my nose up. Saint kills the sound system and leans forward to get a better look.

"Since when the fuck did we eat swanky ass places like this?" I shrug my shoulders and park the rental. We both climb out and walk side by side. His fingers brush against mine and I quickly put some space between us before I do something stupid like, hold his hand! I feel his gaze on me, but ignore it. He has no idea the effect he has on me.

The door is opened for us and immediately the smell of sushi hits me. Fuck yes! I love a good sushi train. I give the woman at the front our names and follow after her. I spot the guys in the back and frown as I look down and check my watch. They said to meet at seven. It's ten to seven, so why the fuck are they all here? When we're within a few feet of them I get it, they gave us the wrong time so we would show up after them.

"Oh shit," Nathan says as he looks up and sees us. Katie has her back to us. I move around the worker lady and step up behind Katie. She tenses the moment I place my hands on top of her shoulders. I look around at all my friends and glower at each of them.

"Imagine my surprise to turn up and see all of you here on time for once?" Leah bites her lip. Corvin glares at me, warning me without words not to make a scene but fuck him, they set us up. "It wasn't until I saw my tatted-up, southern belle, baby momma that I realized you set us the fuck up!" Katie gasps, but I ignore her. Saint slides up beside me as Nathan slowly stands from his chair keeping his murderous gaze on us.

"Nate, please don't," Katie begs.

"Yeah, *Nate*, listen to your girl and sit your ass down," Saint snaps.

"Both of you cut it the fuck out and sit down, now," Darius says. Saint smirks and I shoot him a toothy smile that has the ex-halfback sitting up straighter in his chair.

"So, we can't meddle in any of your relationships but you can meddle in our baby momma drama?" Katie drops her gaze to the table at Saint's words.

"You know what, you both want someone to be pissed at, then be pissed at yourselves," Nathan grits out.

"Shut up, bitch boy. She shacked up with my cousin, I have every right to be pissed." I snarl, drawing a collective gasp around the table.

"Oh, bitch, please. Coming from the guy who showed up an hour after seeing her with him and fucking her brains out in a bathroom?" Beckett chokes on his water, Corvin chokes on fucking air but Darius and the girls just stare at us.

"You're just jealous we weren't fucking you?" Saint teases cockily. Nathan runs his gaze over Saint and shudders dramatically.

"I'd rather drink Katie's cum than touch that limp dick." Everyone groans while Katie buries her face in her hands.

"I can vouch, her cum is delicious," I taunt, and before I can say more, Katie shoves back from the table forcing both Saint and I to move backward. Fire burns in the depths of her eyes and I fucking love it. She thought just because we fucked that it would erase the fact she ran from us.

"You stand here and speak about me like I'm nothing but a common whore. Let's get one thing straight here, shall we, boys?" Saint and I both stand tall and keep our emotionless masks in place. "You want to be pissed at me for leaving? Fine. But let's be honest, shall we? You both lost your shit the moment you found out I was pregnant. When you thought I lost the baby, neither of you came over and held me as I mourned the loss of *our* child." Her voice is rising as her anger begins to peak. "I left because—fuck you both, you don't get to judge me! Go back and live your lives." She looks at me and shakes her head. "You need to stop hiding from who you really are and admit to him that this thing between us worked so well because you don't just love me, you love him too!"

My eyes widen. She turns to Saint next and pins him with a look of disapproval. "And you, stop fucking every cunt that walks past you because no matter how many sluts you bury your cock in, it won't change the fact that you have fallen in love with your best friend! Both of you grow the fuck up and stay the fuck out of my life before you ruin everything!" she screams, garnering the attention of everyone else in the restaurant. Snatching her purse from the back of the chair, she stalks out of the restaurant leaving us here to stare after her.

"I should go. Thank you for dinner," Nathan says as he attempts to go after Katie, but before he can pass us, Saint snaps his arm stopping him. "Move your fucking arm," Nathan snarls.

"What the fuck did she mean when she said *we thought she lost the baby*?" My brows jump to my hairline. I didn't catch that but I'm fucking glad Saint did. Nathan tries to keep his composure but the fact he can't look either of us in the eyes is a tell.

"Nothing. She lost the baby and that's the end of it, now move." Saint drops his arm allowing Nathan to race out of the restaurant. I move to stand in front of him, his gaze boring into mine and I can tell we're both thinking the same thing.

"She lied," he whispers low enough for only me to hear.

"She didn't lose the baby," I answer and he nods.

"We were right, that was milk that squirted out the other night." I nod my head. We thought that was just something common that happened to women after being pregnant but apparently, you only get milk after giving birth so our suspicions were right. "Where the fuck is our baby, Crue?" I grit my teeth and dart my gaze toward the door ready to go after her and demand answers. "We need to do some recon, turns out she may actually really be our baby momma." His words may be meant to reassure me but they don't. Gripping his arm, I lead him away from the others to a corner in the back of the restaurant. The moment we are out of sight of the others, Saint drops his mask. I see the worry and betrayal clear as day on his face.

"If she didn't lose the baby, why did she leave?" I push.

Saint shakes his head and furrows his brows. "I don't know, but Nathan was there and Leah even said she was on Facetime with him and saw the blood. If she didn't lose the baby, how the fuck did she fake that and why?" We both get lost in our thoughts for a minute until Corvin, Darius and Beck come over. They each look us over trying to gauge our mood, but Saint and I are pros at deflecting and using humor to cover our discomfort.

"What happened back there?" Corv asks. I cut a quick glance to Saint to see he has a fake smile plastered on his face.

"Nothing. Crue just wanted me to play with his cock before dinner and I didn't think you guys would like your girls seeing he's twice your size." Darius snorts, Beck rolls his eyes but Corv sees through his bullshit.

"Deflect all you like, asshole, but we know you both better than you think. What the fuck is happening?" Beck pushes, and I see Saint's mask starting to slip. This new turn of events is fucking with him.

"We think Katie lied about losing the baby," I answer for him. The three of them look like a pack of circus clowns with their mouths open and eyes wide. They look how I feel.

"Uh... what?" Corv pushes out, confusion clear on his face.

"Why the hell would you think that? Leah said she lost the baby and was a mess, what would she get out of faking that shit and if she did, where the fuck is the baby?" Darius questions. I'll admit when he says it like that, it does sound far-fetched but I can't shake the feeling that we're right.

"We just have a hunch," Saint says.

"I'm not being a dick, but why do you both care?" I scowl at Beckett. "You both never wanted kids and have made that clear since we were in high school. When you found out she was pregnant neither of you were... happy." What he says is true but we didn't get a chance to even process the idea of having a kid or have time to come to terms with the idea of having a baby before she lost it. We were robbed of that moment, of thinking or even considering the idea of becoming a dad because she waited weeks to tell us the truth. She hid that shit from us and blamed the miscarriage on Saint and me.

"I didn't want kids—I mean, I don't want them but..."

Saint trails off so I cut in and finish his sentence. "The idea of having a kid with her wasn't as bad as we thought. We weren't fucking angry she was pregnant, we were pissed she never told us and hid it from us for weeks. Then before we got the chance to wrap our heads around the idea... she lost the baby." Corvin whistles between his teeth and shakes his head.

"My dudes, you need to tread carefully with this one. If you both go in guns blazing and accuse her of lying about losing the baby only for it to be the truth, she is going to be pissed and fucking hurt. It will bring up emotions I'm sure she has tried to work past, so just be careful on how you approach this."

He's right. I plan to fly home tomorrow and start doing some digging of my own. The moment we get the proof we need, we'll be back to confront our deceitful little southern belle.

CHAPTER FIVE

Katie

I spent the rest of the night fuming and plotting ways I could murder those dumbasses my heart thinks is okay to love! I can't believe they did that shit. Nathan, being the amazing friend he is, brought his mattress into the living room and we spent the remainder of the night watching movies until we fell asleep.

Waking up the next morning, I was hesitant to go to work thinking they would ambush me or the others would, but it turns out, they all really did fly home. I felt lighter after the confirmation from Leah. I can't have them here and have my plans derailed. I need to work on Jackson and getting his phone cloned, that fuckers firewall is impenetrable. Something is off with that though. I've never encountered a firewall that I can't bust through so it tells me he has outside help.

I pull my phone out and bring up my message thread with Jackson.

> Hey, so I was thinking we need a redo of our date....

I start tapping my nails on the counter as I wait for his reply, the guy is odd that's for sure. I had to practically throw myself at him in order to get him to agree to the first date. I mean, don't get me wrong, I don't think I'm God's gift to men but I also know I'm not ugly so I have no idea what his problem is. While I wait for his reply, I bring up my social media app that I have under a fake name, and just as I'm about to click on Saint's profile, I close the app.

"Stop it!" I berate myself. I need to stop doing this. No matter how many times I tell myself I'm over them, I still continue to tear down any news article that paints them in a bad light. Crue doesn't really garner much bad attention but Saint, that is a whole other issue. He's been spotted with numerous different women and it fucking stings each time I see it. And yet, I still hack the news sites and remove the articles anyway. Fuck it, I open the app and go to Crue's profile instead of Saint's only to find it has been removed. Frowning I go to Saint's, and the same thing pops up. Why the hell did they remove their accounts?

My phone finally pings with a reply from Jackson.

JACKSON

Look, Katie, I'm not looking for anything long-term right now. I'm sorry but I don't think it's a good idea.

I stare at the message and reread it several times. I fucking knew something was up with him and this just confirms it. Jackson seeing Saint and Crue clearly spooked him, shit. I scroll my contacts until I find the PI's number and hit dial.

He answers on the fifth ring. "Katie."

"I know I told you to lay low for now but I'm running out of options here, my lead is gone," I admit bitterly.

"I have nothing new to go on, this guy has the money and resources to hide, and without a trail to go on I'm not much help. Have you thought about just going to court?"

"I can't. It's a closed adoption and the agency won't help me. Nothing will stand up in court because I signed away my rights." I swallow past the lump in my throat and close my eyes, willing my tears to remain at bay.

"I'm sorry, Katie, without a lead, I'm not much help and I don't want to keep taking your money when it's wasted without a lead." I thank him and end the call, regret the emotion that is burning strongest inside me right now.

I made the worst decision of my life and now I'm fucking scared I've failed my little girl. I may never get to hold her again, kiss her button nose or brush her blonde hair.

"Fuck this," I snarl. I rush around the store and close up an hour early, if Trent—the owner—asks, I'll just tell him I was sick. I need to see Jackson and do this now. I need those passcodes.

Walking through the front door of his office I garner the attention of most of the workers. I've noticed since I changed my hair color, got a tattoo and stopped smiling all the fucking time that I get judgment from all angles and honestly, I don't give two fucks what anyone thinks of me.

"Miss?" I ignore the women at the front desk as I stroll down the corridor where I know Jackson's office is. "Miss, you can't go back there," she exclaims. I shoot her the bird over my shoulder as I shove Jackson's office door open. His gaze snaps to mine immediately as he holds the phone to his ear, he frowns at the sight of me.

"Uh, Jake, I'm gonna have to call you back," he says as he ends the call. The woman who was shouting at me steps up beside me, shooting me a glare.

"I'm so sorry, I tried to stop her—-" Jackson raises his hand stopping the woman's rambling.

"It's fine, Tessa." The woman huffs and heads out, closing

the door behind herself. Jackson leans back in his chair steepling his hands. He looks like an ignorant prick but I keep my features clear of my disdain for him. "What can I do for you, Katie?" He sounds like a smug prick. How Crue can be related to such a piece of shit I'll never know.

I force myself to smile and act the part of a distraught female who just got her feelings crushed. "I'm just shocked. I thought we had a good time and then… Now you don't want to see me?" I make sure my voice hitches so he thinks I'm on the verge of tears.

"It's a conflict of interest, even going out with you last week I risked my job." I grit my teeth and school my features. This motherfucker only went out to dinner with me in the hopes of getting his dick wet and then ditching me.

This fucker needs a swift kick in the dick.

"I-I thought we had a connection." My bottom lip wobbles, he softens at the sight of it. I mentally high-five myself. He opens his mouth to speak but his office phone rings, sighing he picks up.

"Yes?" he answers, he frowns then nods. "Coming," he says before hanging up and standing. He grabs his suit jacket from the back of his chair and shrugs it on. Fuck, he's going to ask me to leave. "Wait here, I'll be back shortly." I manage to keep the surprised look off my face and smile and nod like a good doe-eyed obedient girl. I spy his phone on his desk and pray he doesn't take it with him. From the way his eyes blaze I can tell he's the type of prick that likes his woman to be seen and not heard, you know the type. "Take a seat." Smiling my thanks, I do as he says, and the moment the door clicks shut behind him, I fist pump the air and quickly pull my laptop from my bag and the cable I'll need. I plugged the cord into his phone and managed to break through his password in seconds and start the cloning process.

I watch the loading circle spin for what feels like hours but is mere seconds before the cloning process starts. I have no idea how long he'll be gone. I tap my foot nervously against the ground as I wait for the data to upload onto my MacBook. I'm taking a huge risk here, if he was to walk in and catch me I have no way to explain what I'm doing. I was supposed to swipe his phone at dinner and do this at home, then drop it to him at work acting like I grabbed his phone by mistake. It's at 90% when I hear voices in the corridor, panic wells inside me. If I stop it now all the data will be wiped and I'll be back to square one!

Fuck!

I hear him right outside the door chatting to someone, it's at 96% now. I want to chew on my nail I'm that fucking nervous. The door handle rattles and I still, I'm busted.

"Jackson, hang on a second," someone calls out. Thank you, Jesus! 100%. I quickly disconnect his phone and place it back where I found it and shove my laptop back in my bag just as the door opens. He heads straight for his desk, grabs his phone then shoots me a disapproving look. Oh my God, he knows and is going to call the cops.

"I have to head into a meeting. I'll need to continue this conversation later." I nod and smile nervously as I stand on wobbly legs.

"Yeah, o-of course," I stutter, earning a frown from him.

"I'll call you." I want to snort, could he not have come up with a better line?

"Do that," I say as I briskly walk my criminal ass out of his office, then out of the fucking building, practically running to my car.

"You've lost your fucking mind!" Nathan shouts and I cringe.

I shoot him a toothy smile. "He didn't catch me," I defend. His eyes narrow as he places his hands on his hips giving me his best disappointed dad glare.

"He could have caught you and then your ass would be in jail! I don't have that type of bail money and let's be real, I'm not that good at sucking dick to convince a judge to not charge you." I can't stop the laughter from bursting out of me, Nathan sucks at telling anyone off. "I'm serious, Katie." My laughter dies in my throat at the hint of concern in his tone. My shoulders droop and my eyes soften as I look at my friend. Everything I have done wouldn't have been possible without his help. I owe him so much and yet he has never asked me for a single thing except to never lie to him.

"I'm sorry. Jackson pulled away from me after seeing Saint and Crue. I had to do something, Nate. I... I can't lose my daughter," I whisper the last part brokenly. He curses under his breath before rushing around the counter in the kitchen to engulf me in a hug. I rest my cheek against his chest and let his embrace ease some of the tension inside me.

"I know, baby girl. Let's order some takeout and we'll spend the night going through all his shit and find our girl." Hearing those words from his mouth has my heart swelling inside my chest.

"Thank you, Nate, for everything you have done and continue to do for me," I mutter.

"I do it because I love your crazy ass."

I chuckle and tighten my hold around his waist. "I love you too."

Nathan orders us takeout while I set up my laptop in the living room and get comfortable on the sofa. I open it and begin to scan through all the emails. Nearly an hour later Nate joins me with our takeout containers. I've scrolled through hundreds of emails and still, I've found nothing. Another hour passes and I'm about ready to give up and cry myself to sleep when Nate comes up with an idea.

"Check the Google Drive, surely he would have his phone linked to his work computer." I do as he says and bring up the drive and gasp. "Is that what I think it is?" Nate whispers from beside me.

"Nate, I think it is," I breathe out. Right here, there are hundreds of files of unscripted adoptions. I never found out Jackson worked for the adoption agency until after I gave birth. The sight of him didn't sit well with me, so I did some digging. That's when I found out, Saint's dad was the one to adopt my baby girl. I knew at that moment it wasn't a coincidence and now I have the proof. Jackson is running off-the-book adoptions.

"Bring up his banking." I do as he says and scroll through his incoming payments. Holy shit. "Is that a payment for a million?" My throat closes up and I nod. "This motherfucker is selling children!"

Horror fills me as I turn to face my friend. "He sold my daughter to Devon. He's going to use my baby girl to black-mail Saint into giving him his company back."

Nate gulps and eyes me warily as he asks, "Didn't you once say that Devon was into some shady shit, like videoing children and selling it on his app?" Bile rushes up my throat as horrible images of what he could be doing to my daughter flash through my mind.

CHAPTER SIX

Saint

Three weeks later

I sit on my bed with my computer in front of me, owning a tech company comes in handy when you have information on people. Since my go-to hacker is no longer in the picture, I've had no choice but to reach out to my staff at my newly named company Morgan Tech IT. Janet has proven herself invaluable when it comes to sourcing Katie's medical records. Grabbing my phone and checking the time, it's nine p.m. here so it's seven in Seattle. Crue should be home from practice now. I dial his number and put it on speaker before bringing up the file Janet just sent me.

"Hey, what's up?"

I smile, I miss talking to him every day. It sucks not being on the same team and being so far away from him but at the end of the day, we knew this could happen and tried to prepare ourselves as much as we could.

"Janet just sent me her medical records," I say.

"Facetime me off your laptop and screen share." I hang up and do as he says. Within a minute his face fills my computer screen, and I share my screen with him as I open the file attached to the email. We're both silent as we read over the notes. I scroll through her records from when she was a child. I stop when I spot a date toward the start of last year in May. She saw Dr. Lordus in Tennessee. This would have been a couple of days after she fled CHU.

"What the fuck is a subchorionic hematoma?" I ask.

"Hold up, let me Google that shit," Crue says as I continue to read on that she was sent home and advised to be on complete bed rest. "Listen to this," Crue says and begins to read out what he found on the internet. "A subchorionic hematoma is when blood collects under the chorion membrane during pregnancy. This membrane attaches the mother's uterine wall to her baby's amniotic sac. The most common symptom is vaginal bleeding. But some people don't have symptoms. Most subchorionic membranes go away on their own without causing pregnancy complications."

"Holy fuck," I breathe out. Crue looks pale and taken aback by the information.

"She didn't lose the baby," he mutters. I ignore him and continue to scroll through the notes. Sure enough, she had ultrasounds booked and regular doctor's appointments to check on the baby because of the hematoma. I stop scrolling when I reach her records from December, right there in bold black print it states that Katie went into pre-term labor. She gave birth on the first of December to a healthy baby girl, weighing in at six pounds two ounces. It looks like the baby had to spend a night being monitored but didn't need to go to the NICU. Crue and I remain silent as we soak in the information we just learned.

We have a baby.

A daughter to be exact.

That thought swirls round and round in my mind for a while, until I try to scroll on and find out more about our child, except it ends. There are no more records of her or our daughter.

"Tonight was my last practice before we break for a few months," Crue says. We didn't make the playoffs but Corvin's team did. I was gutted we didn't make it but after learning this shit, I'm grateful to have a few months off so I can go and strangle the life out of that lying bitch and get my daughter back. "I'm on the next flight to you—"

"Nah, meet back at CHU," I growl.

"Where the fuck was our daughter when she was at dinner? Better yet, who the fuck did she leave her with while we were fucking her at the club?" I shake my head, unable to answer. Something isn't sitting right with me, our girl would be two months old now and there are no records for her at all, my eyes widen when it clicks in my mind.

"She wasn't there."

"I know that asshole, where was she?" he grits out.

"No, you dumbass. She wasn't there because Katie doesn't have her." I stop sharing my screen and then bring up the video of him so he can see me. Crue's face is a mask of confusion, clearly not grasping my meaning so I spell it out for him. "There are no medical reports, Katie didn't have her at the restaurant or anywhere else because the baby isn't in Katie's care." Crue's brows draw in and his eyes burn with anger.

"She gave my fucking daughter away?" he roars. It grates on my nerves that he says *my*, she isn't just his daughter, she's just as much mine as she is his.

"I don't fucking know, we need to dig into this shit more."

"Saint, if she gave away our little girl…" He slams his eyes closed and takes a deep breath. I can see he is warring within himself trying to remain calm.

"Get your ass on a plane first thing tomorrow. I'll meet you back at the house."

"I'll book a red eye for tonight and pick you up in the morning." He sounds defeated and that shit fucks with me, I hate seeing Crue so upset.

"We'll figure this out together."

My fucking back is aching from sitting in that stupid seat for hours. I drag my case after me as I head toward the exit of the airport to meet Crue. It takes me all of two seconds to spot him. He leans against Beck's Audi, with his arms crossed and aviator sunglasses shielding his blue eyes, his blonde hair blowing in the wind.

I frown to myself, was I just checking him out?

I shake that thought away when he spots me and smiles. "Took you long enough," he calls out, smirking. I close the space between us and pull him into a hug. Is it crazy that being here with him, I feel like I can breathe easier?

Crue pulls back and grabs my case off me to put in the trunk as I slip into the passenger seat. He joins me a moment later and within seconds we're driving away, leaving the airport in the rearview mirror. Fuck, it's so good to be home. I didn't realize how much I missed this place until now. All the familiar buildings and parks have me feeling nostalgic.

"I hired that PI guy Troy used." I turn to look at Crue, slightly surprised he took the initiative to do that. Normally he waits for me to call the shots.

"Sweet." Crue lifts his glasses and peers over at me for a second.

"What do you mean *sweet*?"

Shrugging my shoulders, I say, "I don't know, I guess I'm just shocked you did something without me."

Crue snorts and shakes his head. "I stopped needing you to hold my dick a while ago, my man." I force a laugh for his benefit but the truth is, I don't like hearing that he doesn't need me.

What the fuck is wrong with me? Why do I keep acting like a stage-five clinger where he is concerned?

We make small talk all the way back to town, I peer out my window as we pass by our old house and Beck's, pulling into the driveway next door. "What the fuck are you doing?" I ask as I turn to stare at him. He wiggles his brows and smiles wide.

"Welcome home, baby!" he says as he climbs out of the car. Utterly stumped by his meaning, I follow after him and meet his gaze over the roof of the car, quirking a brow.

"The fuck do you mean? Home is next door, asshole."

Crue rolls his eyes and heads toward the trunk to grab my case, then comes to me, grips my hand in his, and begins to skip toward the house, dragging me after him. "This is our new house." I yank my hand free of his just before we reach the porch steps. Crue pauses at the top of the small steps and turns back to me. "Saint, don't overthink this shit, okay? Beck needed a house so he bought one, Darius and Leah live in the old house and in case you didn't know, Corvin bought that one!" He points at the house next to this one and my eyes widen, sure enough, Corvin and Alexa's cars are parked in the driveway.

"So, everyone owns a house on this street but me?" I question as I turn back to him. Hurt flashes in his eyes before he quickly masks it. I mean, what does he expect? How were they able to just buy these houses side by side when they were owned and lived in by others for years? "How did you buy these and get the other owners to agree?"

"Technically, you own this with me, but whatever. We paid nearly triple what they were worth. How could they say no?" he says dejectedly as he spins around and heads inside. I take a moment to take in the house, still in shock. Stepping back I look up to see it's a two-story home, gray and black with white shutters on the windows on the second story. There's a loveseat on the porch and even some potted plants. I slowly make my way inside and freeze the moment I cross the threshold. The decor is all black and gray. Paintings adorn the walls, and pictures of us, the guys and the girls are strate-gically placed around the living area. This house has the same layout as our OG home.

Sure enough, the kitchen is just off the living area, with a pool in the backyard and a games room off the back of the kitchen. I head upstairs expecting the rooms to be in the same order as well, but I'm shocked the moment I hit the second-story landing.

Looking side to side, I see a single room on either side but the sight of the double doors in front of me draws my atten-tion. I slowly creep forward and stop in the doorway at the sight of Crue coming out of some door to the side. At the sight of me pauses.

"Why didn't you tell me you bought a house?" His shoul-ders droop at my question. I move inside the room and look around. There's a large bathroom off to the side, fitted out with a mini hot tub-looking thing, and two walk-in closets on either side of the room, but it's the sight of the California King bed that has questions swirling inside my mind.

"I bought it as a surprise for you and Katie. I was sick of us living apart at the dorms and I knew she wouldn't live next door after what happened. I wanted to surprise you both with this, I thought this house could be our fresh start to really make things official between us and actually make this… thing between us work, then everything turned to shit."

Guilt rears its ugly head inside me. I close the space between us and rest my hands on top of his shoulders and smile, hoping it may ease some of the tension. "I'm fucking surprised, that's for sure." We both chuckle but I can tell he's still upset at how I reacted. "The house is fucking dope. I guess I always thought we'd buy our first home together." His eyes spark with an unreadable emotion.

"You wanted to buy a house with me?" I shrug, trying to play off the warmth I feel building inside me.

"It's always been me and you, Crue. Yeah, we have the guys and now the girls, but from day one, it's always been us. You're my fucking ride or die. I can't do any of this shit without you." His eyes soften for a second before a lustful look overtakes his blue eyes and I'm stumped as fuck as to where that look is coming from.

What happens next is something I never saw coming. Crue smacks my hands away, grips the back of my neck and pulls me to him. Before I can process what is happening, his lips are on mine, then his tongue is inside my mouth.

CHAPTER SEVEN

The moment the taste of him hits my senses I growl. Fuck, I never thought this moment would ever happen and now that it's here, I'm nervous as fuck. When he lifts his arms, I expect him to push me away so, to save myself from the heartache I break the kiss and step back. We're both breathing hard and fast, his eyes wide with shock. That's when I realize what the fuck I just did. I crossed a line that I never should have. I open my mouth to try to defend my actions but he beats me to it.

"I'm not gay." Fuck! Any hope I ever had of being with him flees my body. "But, I'm rock-fucking-hard right now." My brows hit my hairline, and before I can say anything Saint is on me, his lips on mine, and he doesn't go slow. He forces his tongue inside my mouth. One hand grips the back of my neck while the other grips my waist and holds me in place. I grab fistfuls of his shirt, pull him closer and deepen the kiss. Fuck, the moment he thrusts forward I can feel how hard he is for me and I gasp into his mouth. Saint spins and then shoves me backward until I fall on the bed, he stands towering over me with a hunger in his green eyes I've never seen before. "I have no idea what the fuck is happening right now, all I know is it's going to happen if you don't stop it now."

I shake my head. "I don't want to stop it," I answer honestly. I've wanted this for years and if he's finally willing to admit that he wants me as much as I want him, I'm not going to deny him.

"Okay." He's nodding like he's warring within himself on if he should continue or not. "I've never… this is new to me." The vulnerability in his voice has me softening.

"I've never done this either." His face contorts in confusion.

"Really?"

Rolling my eyes I answer, "Yeah, really, dick."

He reaches up and rubs the back of his neck looking slightly sheepish. "I mean… I just assumed because you—"

"No, asshole. I'm not into guys. I'm just… into you." I don't know how to explain it. Saint is the only male I've ever wanted and that hasn't changed for years. Don't get me wrong, I love pussy but there is something about Saint that draws me in every time and I'm powerless to stop it.

"Uh, same." Well shit, that shocks me. Rather than make this shit awkward and risk him backing out, I sit up and pull my shirt off tossing it to the side. Saint's eyes widen for a second before he ditches his own shirt. Both of us take the other in before we both rid ourselves of our pants. I stand and slowly let my eyes devour him as he did me. It's not like we haven't seen each other naked or anything like that, but there was always Katie there and now, it's just us. There is no hiding my feelings for him at this moment. Am I fucking terrified? Yes. I don't want this to fuck up what we have, he's my best friend and I won't risk losing that. "Lose them." The authority in his voice has me obeying without complaint.

I push my boxers down my legs and kick them to the side, without thinking I step forward and hold his gaze as I push his boxers down his legs. The moment his cock springs free, I grip it in my hand and relish in the hiss that escapes him. I tentatively begin to pump him and smirk proudly when his eyes roll back and he drops his forehead against mine, moaning. A fucking girly gasp rips from me when he grips my cock. Jesus, I've envisioned what it would feel like to have his hand on my dick for years, but none of that compares to the real thing.

"Fuck," I grit out as he continues to pump faster. At this rate, I'm about to bust a nut before we can do anything else. Saint shifts so he can meet my gaze, the hungry look that shines in his eyes fuels my desire for him. He claims my lips in a kiss that robs me of breath. Fuck, he's such a beast. I love how he fights to prove he's the one in control, even if it's taking control of the kiss or making sure he's the one pumping my cock faster.

Breaking the kiss and releasing me he shoves me again until I'm flat on the bed. "Lube?"

I shake my head and push my excitement at the fact this is actually happening out of my mind so I can answer him. "Side drawer." Nodding, he opens the drawer and grabs the bottle out, then turns back to me.

"Are you sure?" The tenderness in his tone fucking melts me.

"Yeah," I answer without hesitation.

"Turn over." I do as he says and wait with bated breath. I hear him squirt the lube and then his hands are gripping my ass cheeks and parting them to apply a generous amount of lube to my asshole, a groan pulls from me at the feeling of him prodding my ass with his finger. "Fuck, Crue, I'm not gonna be able to be gentle, I'm too fucking hard for that." I look over my shoulder at him.

"Fuck me, Saint." I never thought I would get the chance to say those three little words. My mouth waters at the sight of him lubing his thick cock. The moment he flicks his gaze to mine, arousal surges through me knowing he's rock-fucking-hard for *me*. He steps up behind me and as much as I want this, I still tense. I've never done this before and contrary to what everyone thinks, getting fucked in your ass hurts—Katie told me. Saint runs his hand up and down my back trying to ease some of the tension.

"Relax." I take a deep breath and try to do as he says. "If it's too much, just say and we stop, okay?" I nod. Truth is, even if it hurts like a bitch, I would never deny him this. I've wanted this for too long to allow some pain to get in the way of this moment. "The fucking words, Crue, you know I need them."

The dominance in his tone has a shiver rolling down my spine. "Yes."

"Good," is all he says before the head of his cock is pressing against my hole. I breathe through the burn and force myself to relax as much as I can. "Fuck, that's tight." I grunt in response as he continues to slowly ease his way inside me. Fuck, the burn is crippling, I'm gripping the comforter in a vice-like grip and grinding my teeth. He stops pushing inside my ass and slowly draws back only to thrust inside me softly. He continues to do this until I'm moaning and relaxed enough for him to continue slipping further inside me without much pain. The moment he's balls deep in my ass we both groan. "Fuck, Crue, I need to fuck you, can you take it?"

"Fuck yes!" A sheen of sweat coats my entire body. Saint grips my hips in a vice-like hold and begins to fuck me. Holy shit, the feelings inside me are none I've ever experienced before. The harder he fucks me and hits the G-spot inside my ass, I can't help the sounds that come from me. "Saint," I shout as he continues to hit that spot over and over again.

"Fuck yes," he growls, then reaches around me to grip my cock. I jerk against him as he continues to fuck me and pump my cock. "Get there, Crue, I'm about to come."

"Keep going, don't fucking stop." He obeys my demand

and continues to thrust inside me until a white haze over takes my vision as I cum harder than I ever have before whilst yelling his name and coming in his hand.

"Crue," Saint roars as his own orgasm crashes through him and he comes in my ass. Shudders tear through both of us as we slowly come down from our high. Saint flops forward against my back, both of us panting and trying to catch our breath. We stay like this until our breathing even outs. Saint shifts and I flinch. "Fuck, sorry. I'm gonna pull out."

"Okay." He pulls out slowly and fuck it stings like a bitch. I push off the bed and head straight for the bathroom so I can shower. The moment I step under the spray, Saint enters wearing his jeans and a look of unease on his face. Thanks to it being an open shower, I have no problem seeing him. "Just say whatever is on your mind," I say as I begin to wash myself. I cringe when I feel his cum begin to leak out of my ass. That's a feeling I don't think I will ever get used to.

"Look, that was fucking amazing and everything but..." He lets his sentence travel off. I wash quickly, then shut the shower off before snagging a towel off the rack, wrapping it around my waist, before turning to face my best friend, who looks like he's on the verge of having a breakdown.

"It was a one-time thing." His brows raise. "Don't get me wrong, I've wanted that for years but if I'm being honest with myself and you, since meeting Katie, shit shifted." He nods. "Do I love you?" He tenses and his face becomes an emotionless mask. "Fuck yes, you're my best friend but you're also just... more." I can't explain this thing between me and Saint. Was it fucking amazing? Yes, but now that the itch has been scratched so to speak, I now know it was never about being with him physically.

A whoosh of air escapes him and he smiles wide. "Same, I love you too." The tension that was present a second ago is now gone. The divide I felt between us for months is also gone and fuck it feels good to have no barrier between us again. I now know that wedge was put there because I wasn't the only one who had feelings, but Saint didn't know how to act on them. Without her we are struggling… we are nothing… we aren't complete. We thought us having sex would fix the hole she left but it didn't. The sound of my phone ringing has me rushing out of the bathroom and back into the bedroom to fish it out of my jeans.

I answer the call and bring It to my ear. "Yeah?"

"Crue Hastings?" I tense at the tone in the caller's voice. Half expecting it to be some crazy fan confessing their undying love for me.

"Who's asking?" I growl. Saint comes to stand in front of me with a worried look on his face.

"My name is Carlos. Troy told me you were looking for information and given the fact his regular PI is helping the person you are searching for he thought it better to refer you to me." I place the call on speaker so Saint can hear.

"So, Katie has a PI? Why?" Saint frowns and I mouth I'll tell him later.

"She is looking into the adoption of her daughter." My blood turns to ice and Saint turns pale as Carlos confirms what we had speculated.

"How the fuck did she put her up for adoption without our consent?" Saint snarls.

Carlos doesn't question the fact that Saint spoke and not me, he just answers his question. "The father signed the adoption papers." We both exchange a loaded look.

"We didn't sign shit," I say.

"The paperwork I've managed to procure shows the father's signature, he signed his rights away the day the child was born."

"Send me the fucking paperwork," Saint demands.

"Can you find out who adopted her?" I ask.

"I'm working on it now. The file is just downloading. This

was a closed adoption so it's been hard getting any information on this case. Something isn't right with it."

"What do you mean?" I push.

"This adoption wasn't put through the right channels. I mean there is paperwork to prove it but it was rushed and the family wasn't vetted. It's like they knew someone in the agency or paid them off." Dread pools inside me. Saint looks like he might hurl and I don't blame him.

"So, Katie never met the family she gave our daughter to?" Saint whispers.

"By the looks of it, no. The agency dealt with all of that but I can also see that Katie has put in numerous requests to find out more information, but she signed her rights over and has no claim to the child."

"She may have no rights but we didn't sign over shit. I want my daughter," Saint snaps.

"Uh, gentlemen, we may have a problem."

"What is it?" I hedge.

"I'm going to assume that is Saint Morgan with you?" Both of us frown.

"Uh, yeah, why?" I grit out.

"Turns out, Katie, didn't give the baby to just anyone after all," he says.

"What the fuck does that mean?" Saint snaps, clearly at his wits end with this call.

"Devon Morgan is listed as the guardian for the child. Your father adopted your daughter." And just like that, everything inside me dies. Saint drops to his knees and cradles his face in his hands as he begins to scream.

CHAPTER EIGHT

Katie

It's been weeks and still I have fucking nothing!

I can't find Devon anywhere. I'm broke and have no money to pay someone else to help me track this fucker down. My grades have slipped, but I can't find it within myself to care that I'm failing school. I'm at the point where I'm ready to curl into a ball and stay there. I've fucked up so badly. I should have told them about Adalyn and maybe they would have been able to help, but I was too stupid and hurt by their rejection of her to even reach out. My bedroom door slams and I shriek in fright. Nathan stands there with a pale face and terrified look in his eyes.

"What is it?" I ask as I leap off the bed and rush to him.

"You need to see this," he says as he grabs my arm and drags me from my room into the living room. He grabs the remote and presses play on the TV. A news reporter appears and my eyes widen at the picture of Saint that pops up in the background.

'Seattle Seahawks running back, BCD'S and Morgan Tech IT owner, Saint Morgan has released a statement claiming that his father, Devon Morgan has adopted his daughter illegally and urging

anyone with information to come forward as he is offering a hundred-thousand-dollar reward for any information…

Everything becomes white noise as I turn to Nathan with wide eyes. "He knows about her," I breathe out.

He nods. "He's searching for him. I called Leah and apparently he and Crue have been searching for her since they arrived back at CHU a few days ago." Fear grips me in its clutches.

"If they know about her, that means they know what I did," I whisper.

"You need to get your ass on a plane and get back there. The three of you together will be able to bring your little girl home, baby girl."

I shake my head. "They hate me, they will never let me—"

"They left you!" he shouts. My eyes widen because Nathan never loses his cool. "You did what you had to! Pack your shit, we're leaving tonight."

I get choked up as I look at my friend. "Y-you're gonna come with me?"

His eyes soften. "I would never let you face this on your own, plus, if they know about her then they know about me signing the papers so I need to answer for that." Shame and guilt wash over me.

"They'll never forgive you," I sob. "I had no right asking you to do what I did."

"Hush, you didn't ask me to do shit. Go pack, I'll book us some flights."

"I can't afford the airfare," I mutter.

"Well, lucky for you I have sugar daddies who love my Only Fans. This one's on me, boo." I owe Nathan so much. I couldn't have done any of this without him. Nerves thrum through me at the prospect of facing the guys. I know them and I know they are going to lash out and blame me for everything. Honestly, I can't blame them because this is all my fault.

Nathan and I sit in the back of the Uber not saying a word. Even though he reassures me he is fine and not worried, I can tell from how tense he is and by his lack of snarky remarks, he's just as nervous as I am to be back here. The closer we get to the old house, the clammier my hands get. I have to keep wiping them on my denim shorts. The moment we pull down the street, my breathing picks up. We pass Beck's house and the Uber pulls up next to the curb of the house where my whirlwind romance with the two guys who turned my life upside down began.

We grab our bags and stand on the curb looking at the house like it's going to suddenly start cussing us out or something. "You ready?" Nate asks.

Sighing I shake my head. "No, not really." Before more can be said the front door opens and Leah is rushing toward us. I can't help but smile at the sight of her. She launches herself at us and squeals as she wraps each of her arms around our necks and pulls us in. I melt into her. I fucking missed her so much.

"Oh my God, I'm so happy you're here," Leah says, pulling back and beaming at us. I spy Darius over her shoulder, making his way toward us.

"Katie!" I dart my gaze to the right to see Val rushing toward us from her house with Beck and Dawson following after her. Nathan and I greet each of the guys, and Val. Dawson has grown so much since I last saw him. "Come on, let's go inside—" Val's cut off from the shout coming from our left.

"You motherfucker!"

"You're a dead man, bitch," Crue and Saint both shout as they run toward us. I stumble back scared shitless at the sight of the looks on their faces. I knew they would be mad but I never expected them to come for me like this. Darius and

Beck rush in front of me, Nate steps up beside me as Leah ushers Val and Dawson back so they don't get hurt. The moment they are within reach they don't stop like I thought they would, Saint leaps off the ground and practically lands on Darius's shoulder as his fist connects with Nathan's cheek sending him backward. I scream as I rush toward my friend only to be shoved backward and land on my ass as Crue jumps on top of Nate and lands punch after punch to his face and body. Nate doesn't just take it, he fights back with everything he has and lands a few good hits to Crue's jaw and ribs.

"Stop them!" I scream. Beck rushes forward to grab Crue off Nathan while Darius holds Saint back, I can see Darius is struggling and I begin to panic. Beck manages to pull Crue off Nate. Without thinking, I crawl across the grass and lay over my bestie trying to protect him just as Saint breaks free of Darius's hold with his fist in the air, I slam my eyes closed ready to take the hit for Nate.

"Saint!" At the sound of Crue's panicked shout, I slowly open my eyes one at a time to see Saint's fist an inch from my face, his eyes wide with shock.

"Are you outta your fucking mind?" Saint roars, causing me to flinch. Nate tries to push me off him so I'm out of harm's way just as Saint drops his arm back to his side. I smack his hands away and remain where I am, not daring to move in case they attack my friend again. "Answer me, Katie."

I scowl up at the entitled prick. "Fuck you. You had no right to do that to him—-"

"Get fucked!" Saint seethes as Crue pulls out of Beck's hold to stand next to him and glare down at me.

"That cunt signed away our rights to our daughter." My eyes widen and I swallow audibly. "You think you can come back here and talk to us like you have a fucking right after what you did?" Crue doesn't give me a chance to answer. "You and your fake-ass baby daddy need to get the fuck out of here and stay the fuck away from us. When we get *our* daughter back you won't be welcome in her life." Tears spring to my eyes at his callous words. He has no idea what the fuck I went through or the struggle I faced with this decision.

"I did what I had to do to help *her*," Nathan shouts from beneath me.

"We didn't even fucking know the baby existed!" I shrink into Nathan at the angry lilt of Saint's voice.

"If you both hadn't acted like dicks when you found out about the pregnancy, she would have told you," Nate tries to defend me but I know it's futile. The looks on their faces tell me that nothing Nate or I say will change the hatred they feel toward us and what we did.

"She fucking lied! When she found out she didn't lose the baby she should have come clean but instead, she hid from us and sold our kid!" The emotion in Crue's voice can be felt. I know I fucked up but I'm not going to be subjected to their judgment when they weren't there and have no idea what fucking struggles I faced. Gritting my teeth, I push to my feet and look to each of these entitled assholes who think they have the right to stand there and look down their noses at me.

"You both screamed and shouted when you found out I was pregnant, then when you thought I had lost the baby I saw the relief in each of your eyes. So don't you dare fucking stand there and act like I did something wrong! You both told me I would never be a good mother, you made me feel like I was worthless and could never be a good mother to my own daughter, so fuck you both." I feel Nathan at my back ready to defend me if they decide to come at me again. This wasn't how I wanted this to play out. Neither of them says a word for a minute but they don't need to, the look in their eyes says everything their mouths can't.

They hate me. I've tried to convince myself for months that I hate them just as much but the truth is, even after everything they have done to me my heart can't help but still beat for them!

Saint begins to nod and takes a step back. He reaches out and grips Crue's arm, pulling him with him until they're nearly back on their driveway. "Do you, Katie baby, we'll get our daughter back and make sure to send you a picture of her once every ten years." Pain radiates inside my chest. Nathan growls from behind.

"Neither of you deserves Adalyn," Nathan shouts. Crue and Saint still.

"You named her?" Crue asks in a deathly calm tone that has me tensing.

I dart my tongue out to moisten my lips and nod. "Yes," I grit out.

"What'd you name her?" Saint asks in a tone void of all emotion except one, disgust.

Taking a deep breath, I hold my head high and square my shoulders as I meet their stares. "Adalyn Faith Hastings-Morgan." Both their jaws lock. Crue nods before turning and storming back into the house. Saint lingers for a minute, just staring at me with a blank look on his face. I hate the distance between us, I step forward and hope to hell he doesn't push me away when I close the space between us and stop a foot away from him. His breathing is erratic, his eyes now burn with unease at my close proximity. "Want to see a picture of her?" I ask hesitantly. The moment his shoulders droop and his brows raise I decide not to wait for an answer and just show him. Pulling my phone from my pocket I unlock it and show him my wallpaper.

Snatching the phone from my grasp he brings it closer to his face to stare at our little one. "She's beautiful," he whispers brokenly. I open my mouth to voice my agreement but I don't get a chance to utter a word as he grips my arm and pulls me after him. I don't fight him, not even when Nathan begins shouting my name and spewing threats at Saint. They won't hurt me. Well, not physically but I can't guarantee they won't obliterate what's left of my heart. He shoves the front door open, and pushes me inside before slamming and locking the door behind us. His eyes drill into me. The moment they begin to darken, I swallow and back up as he slowly prowls toward me. I shriek when I smack into something—no, not something, someone. The moment Crue's arms band my middle and pull me back against him, I melt. I should be screaming for help and trying to get free but the truth is, I'm so tired of running and I know now, I can't do this on my own. I need them.

I've always needed them.

Saint closes the space between us, his front is plastered against mine. My body begins to heat at their nearness, my senses are going haywire as memories of the last time we fucked swirl through my mind. I bite my lip to stop the groan that wants to break free. Crue buries his face in the crook of my neck, inhaling my scent and drawing a gasp from me, Saint grips my chin and lifts my face until I meet his gaze.

"You had us, everything that we are and were to become was yours." Saint's words have me stilling and dread pooling inside me. "You broke our hearts when you ran." A lump forms in my throat and tears cloud my vision as I stare up at him. "Thing is, we started to deal with your loss until we found out you took something of ours with you when you fled." His grip on my chin hardens, Crue's hold around my waist turns punishing. "Now, we'll do everything in our power to bring our girl home." The relief I feel is short lived the moment Crue whispers in my ear.

"You fucked up badly giving our girl to Saint's daddy. Because of that fuck up, you will pay. You will never see her again. She'll never know who you are, what you look like, the sound of your voice. But, don't worry, we'll make sure we find her a new mommy that will love her better than the disgrace that gave birth to her." In unison they both leap away from me and leave me standing here as tears trail down my cheeks, and a hollow feeling takes hold of me. Once again, I'm left standing alone to deal with the pain they have caused me. I'm a fool for thinking that they would help me get her back. All they want to do is hurt me and make me feel the pain they felt when I left. Newsflash, assholes, I felt the exact same pain they did when they left me in a pool of my own blood the night I thought I miscarried.

CHAPTER NINE

Saint

Three days later

Crue, Troy, Beckett, Darius and even Corvin have joined us via video feed as we all sit around the living room in mine and Crue's house. All we have done for three days is hunt down my father. With all the resources we have managed to get in contact with one of his old pals who was all too willing to give up my father's hiding place. Devon shouldn't have fucked over his friend, then he wouldn't have snitched out his location.

"Even though there was a rush, the adoption is still legal. I've petitioned the courts to have this fast-tracked given that the birth certificate was forged by Nathan." I grit my teeth at Troy's words. The moment I get my hands on Nathan, he is fucking done.

"I'm not going to sit here and do nothing while my daughter is stuck with that cunt." I grunt my agreement, Crue and I both agreed the moment we found out the location of Adalyn we would go get her and now we have that.

"'In the eyes of the law, he is the father—"

I cut Troy off. "Like fuck he is! That's my daughter and

either you get the fuck to the courthouse now and revoke his rights or I put a bullet in his fucking head. You choose." Everyone stares at me like I've lost my mind. Hey, I might have, but right now I don't give a fuck. I just want my girl home where she is safe. Darius and Beck climb to their feet and shoot Troy an apologetic look.

"Sorry T-man," Darius says with a shrug before looking at me. "How many of us are flying to New Zealand?" I cut a glance to Crue. He's stiff and clearly mulling over Darius's words, unsure what the fuck to do.

"Crue?" I hedge. He shakes his head to clear his thoughts, his blue eyes boring into me.

"We have to take the egg donor with us," he grits out through clenched teeth. I take a ragged breath through my nose at the thought of seeing Katie. we haven't seen the dirty lying bitch since she ran out of here three days ago.

"Val won't like it but she has to stay back. I won't have my son near any of this." Crue and I both nod, the last thing we want is our nephew anywhere near my scum fuck of a father. "I'll make sure Val has whatever you need for the baby here when we get back." We both thank Beck. Out of all of us, he and Val are the only ones with experience with kids, well, Val more so than Beck.

"There is no fucking way jail bait is going, her crazy ass is staying here," Corvin chimes in from behind us where we have him synced to the TV. "You both know if you need me, I'm on the first flight—"

Crue cuts Corvin off. "Nah, man, stay your ass there and win us that game so we can go to the Super Bowl." A wide grin stretches across Corv's face.

"Who gets to tell Goldie she can't come? Becky?" We all stare at Darius, the guy looks like the ultimate bad boy and throws off all those dark and dangerous vibes, but when it comes to Leah, the guy is a fucking pussy.

Beck snorts and shakes his head. "You're on your own, *halfback*," he mocks D, using Leah's nickname for him.

Darius runs a hand through his hair and looks toward the TV. "Corv, my man—"

"Eat a dick, Darius," Corvin says before he can finish. D sighs and nods. Truthfully, out of the girls Alexa and Leah are the fucking crazy ones, so I don't blame him for being worried about telling his girlfriend she can't come with us.

"If the egg donor has to come, maybe Leah should tag along," Crue interjects. Darius's eyes light up with gratitude.

"Fucking love ya, my man," D shouts, earning an eye roll from the rest of us.

"Troy, fast track the court," I say. He nods and gathers his things to head out. "We need the egg donor to do her thing and hack into whatever it is to get us a passport made to bring our girl home." I'm about to say Crue and I will go speak to her but Beck beats me to it.

"I'll speak to her now. Book the flights for tomorrow night. I need tomorrow morning to get the house installed with more cameras while we're gone." Beck looks to Corv next. "I want Alexa with Dawson and Val while we're away."

"Agreed, I'll tell her," Corv says without hesitation. I know this is hard for them both, being away from their girls after everything that happened with Cody, but this is what brotherhood is. They're both scared to leave but will do it anyway because we asked them, this is what family is.

Blood doesn't make you family. Love and loyalty do!

I roused awake from the sound of Crue's phone ringing. I roll over and have to use my leg to kick him awake—this fucking bed is huge. He groans and tries to roll away so I throw the pillow at his dumb ass. He jolts upright and looks around the room in a panic—he's always been a fucking deep sleeper.

"Answer that fucking thing so I can sleep!" He grunts in answer and reaches blindly for his phone. He answers the call without checking who it is.

"What?" I smirk. Crue fucking hates being woken up unless it's game day or for sex. I see him tense and then I'm scooting across the bed to rip the phone from his grasp and put it on speaker.

"—I can't afford the ticket to New Zealand—"

I growl before cutting in to shut her ass up. "Tickets are booked, get the passport made and don't be fucking late. We booked your ass to sit in the cargo hold with all the other bags." I end the call and toss Crue's phone onto his lap. He tosses it back on the bedside table before laying back down. I do the same but this time, I can't fucking sleep. That bitch fucking ruined my good night's sleep with her ringing at the ass crack of dawn. Crue sighs from beside me, I know he's thinking the same thing as I am.

"What do we do when we get back?" he asks quietly

"We'll cross that bridge when we come to it."

He rolls onto his side and faces me. "Devon won't let this go, Saint. He's going to take us to court." I mimic his move and roll over to face him, there's still a large space between us thanks to the size of the bed.

"I know. We just need to get her away from him and then we worry about all the other shit later."

"Does that shit include the mother of our kid?" A whoosh of air escapes me. I know to others it may sound weird, Crue and I referring to Adalyn as *ours*, but it isn't for us. I don't need to find out which one of us is her father, I'd love her regardless because I love him.

"If I say no, will you believe me?" A light laugh escapes him.

"I guess we'll deal with that when we get back as well, huh?"

"Shut the fuck up and go to sleep."

Crue and I wait at the gate for the others to arrive, neither of us wanted to be near Katie for longer than we had to so we drove ourselves. I'm fucking thankful him and I were able to work shit out between us and return to how things were before she went and ran, but now, I can feel this gap in our lives and I fucking hate that I know she is the only one who can fill that void.

"Why the fuck is he here?" I look up from my phone at Crue's voice and frown at the sight of Nathan with Darius, Beck, Leah and Katie. Pocketing my phone, Crue and I both head toward them but before we can get near Nathan, Katie jumps in front of us and places her hands on each of our chests like she has a right to touch us after what she fucking did!

"Don't you dare hurt him," she snarls. Narrowing my eyes at her, I make sure she can see that her pathetic pleas mean nothing to me anymore. "He helped me. If you need an explanation about why I did what I did we have a long ass flight and have the time. None of this is what either of you think—"

"How the fuck would you know what we think?" Crue cuts in and asks.

Katie doesn't cower away from his harsh tone. "I know you love Saint. I also know he loves you but didn't know how to show you without using me to do it." My eyes widen slightly before I quickly school my features. "I can also see that you both finally gave into your... urges—" Before she can finish I slap a hand over her mouth and pin her with a warning look to shut her fucking mouth.

"You have the plane ride to convince us not to murder him. Fail to do so and your wannabe baby daddy will be lying in a ditch somewhere in New Zealand," I snarl. I cut a quick glance to Nathan who stands there stoically behind

Darius and Beck. Fucking pussy, I think as I pull away and head for the gate to get this flight over with.

The flight attendant leads us to our seats in first class. Crue leads while Katie is in the middle of us. I watch her look around and take everything in. She's too busy looking around to notice Crue has stopped and bumps into him. She stumbles backward only to knock into me, so I grip her waist to steady her. She clears her throat and quickly rights herself before mumbling her thanks and moving to the middle seat the hostess points out. I snag the one on her other side so she's stuck sitting between Crue and me.

"If there's anything you need, please let me know," the stewardess says, and before she can leave Katie's words stop her.

"I need to express, do you have somewhere where the milk can be stored so I can donate it?" I peer around her pod to stare at Crue who is looking directly at me. This bitch.

The hostess opens her mouth but I cut on before she can answer. "She's joking, don't worry about it." Katie turns toward me, ready to argue but whatever she sees on my face has her clamping her mouth closed and slouching back in her seat.

Crue leans across the aisle, Katie tenses as she meets his angry stare. "You aren't giving away my kids fucking food. Put it in a container or keep it in your tits if you have to, but you aren't giving it away."

"I can't keep it in, you dick," she whisper shouts. "I have to express every two hours, so unless you plan on drinking it and storing it in your nut sacks for later use, I have to pump it and dump it." Crue's face screws up in disgust.

"You aren't dumping shit or giving it away," I interject. she shoots both of us a scathing look before crossing her arms over her chest. I see her flinch and that's when I pay closer attention. Her tits look fuller, almost like they have grown two cup sizes. She doesn't notice me watching as she gently massages the tops of her tits and the side, almost like she is trying to relieve the pressure of her milk. Fuck, the longer I stare at her the more I see she isn't just uncomfortable—-she's in pain. She keeps her eyes closed and continues to rub her tits as the plane takes off, and the moment we are in the air and the captain turns the seatbelt sign off, I'm on my feet and yanking her to hers.

"What are you doing?" she snaps in an annoyed tone.

"Get whatever the fuck you need to empty your tits and follow me." Relief shines in her eyes. She grabs her backpack off the floor and motions for me to lead the way. I shoot Crue a look to follow us as I lead the way toward the bathroom, benefits of first class is the bathrooms are big enough to fit the three of us with ease.

CHAPTER TEN

Katie

Crue shuts and locks the door. I stand here awkwardly with my bag clutched against my chest as the two of them stand there staring at me with bored looks on their faces. When it becomes obvious that they plan on staying while I do this, I balk at them.

"Seriously?" I hiss. Crue crosses his arms over his chest while Saint quirks a brow daring me to push this matter. "Fine," I grit out as I close the toilet seat lid and place my bag on top of it. As I grab out the pump and all its connections, I turn to the side and thank the lord above that the bathroom has a power socket. I plug it in and turn my back to the guys as I lift my shirt over my head and unclasp my bra, when I hear a hiss and groan come from them, it fills me with warmth to know that they still enjoy the sight of me. I flinch in pain when I secure the cups to each of my nipples. I didn't have time to express before we left the house, I'm so full and it fucking hurts. I switch on the pump and sigh the moment it begins to pull the milk from me.

I never knew how painful it felt for your breasts to fill with milk. If you don't get relief from expressing or feeding the baby, it's fucking agony having them this full. I know I'm gonna be here for a while and need to change out the bottles to the other ones to relieve myself so I move my bag to the floor and turn around before dropping down onto the lid of the toilet. Both their eyes widen at the sight of the contraption attached to me. I cross my leg over the top of the other and try to look as sexy as one can with this shit attached to their tits and say,

"Welcome to my daily life. Well, actually this is what I do every couple hours. You want answers from me so ask what you want to know. I'm gonna be here awhile emptying these bad bitches out." They narrow their eyes at the snarky tone of my voice, but I'm passed caring what they think.

"Why'd you lie to us about losing her?" Crue asks. I refuse to cower under the pressure of his gaze, sitting up straight as I answer.

"I didn't." He opens his mouth to argue but I push on. "I really did think I lost the baby. I bled everywhere and anyone with a brain knows when you're pregnant and bleed it means you lost the baby. After the night you both came over and found the test and we fought, I thought I lost her then and that's when I decided that I needed to head home. I had to get away and try to recover from the loss of Cody and everything you two did to me, except, before I could leave, I fainted and thought it was due to blood loss. Turns out I didn't lose the baby."

"What happened?" Saint asks.

"I found out that I had a subchorionic hematoma and bleeding is normal with that. I was shocked as hell to learn I was still pregnant. I thought I had for sure lost the baby after all the stress and everything with losing Cody and the night we all argued when you found out."

"You ran from us!" I glare at Crue.

"I didn't have a choice, you both left me! I was spiraling, couldn't you fucking see that? My best friend was murdered. I wanted to tell you both about the baby but then shit with

Corvin happened and it never felt like the right time. Then, I thought I lost her. I blamed myself for losing our baby. If I had of put her first instead of living in my own grief of losing my best friend she would be fine. Neither of you two were fucking there, so don't you dare judge me!"

"You should have told us you found out you didn't lose the baby," Saint roars. I flinch at the sound of his angry tone and drop my gaze to my lap.

"You're right, I should have told you both but I couldn't," I whisper.

"Why?" I mull over Crue's question for a minute debating if I should lie but what good would that do?

I slowly lift my head and look to each of them. God, they're so beautiful even when they look at me with nothing but anger and distrust. "Look how you both reacted when you found that test, neither of you two were happy. I mean, for God's sake, Crue, you blamed me for getting pregnant and made out like I planned this!" I shake my head and look to Saint next. "And you, how could you accuse me of sleeping with you both for a golden ticket to a life where I would never have to struggle?" They both at least have the decency to look appalled by their actions. "Don't bullshit me and say you weren't relieved when you thought I lost the baby, so forgive me for not calling my boyfriends with the amazing news of finding out that our daughter wasn't dead and in fact alive and thriving inside me."

"Boyfriends, huh?" I growl.

"Seriously, Crue? Out of everything I just said that's all you heard?" Saint nudges him with his shoulder, telling him without words not to be a dick.

"Regardless, Katie. That baby is ours and we had a fucking right to know about her existence!" I shrink back at the venom in Saint's tone. "You got that fucking bitch Nathan to fake being her father and gave my baby girl away!" He's shouting now and I begin to worry everyone else in first-class will be able to hear our argument. "Did you fucking know you signed her over to the fucking devil himself?"

Shame washes over me. I shake my head and quickly reach into my bag to grab the spare bottles and place them on the counter next to the sink. Switching the pump off while I try to unscrew the bottle. After the third attempt I growl, then gasp when Saint knocks my hands out of the way and unfastens the bottle for me. "Thanks," I mumble as I screw the lid on and quickly replace it with the empty bottle. I do the same to the other side before switching the pump back on.

"What do you do with all that milk?" Crue's question shocks me. I manage to snap out of it and answer him as I reclaim my seat.

"I donate it to the local hospital back home."

"Answer my question," Saint snaps. I steel my spine and hold their gazes as I spill the story.

"No, I had no idea about your father. I met with someone from the adoption agency not long after I found out I was still pregnant. Believe me if I knew that cocksucker was the one who would adopt her, I never would have gone through with it."

"Why the fuck did you give her up?" Crue snarls.

I pin him with a scathing look daring him to come at me again. "I couldn't fucking afford to raise her, okay? The moment my family found out I was pregnant out of wedlock, my ass was kicked to the curb. I moved in with Nathan and had to drop back on classes at school so I could work. I make fucking shit money at my job, I could barely get by as it was. I never wanted her to suffer because I couldn't provide shit for her—"

"We would have paid for everything!" Saint interjects.

"You weren't there!" They both recoil at my shout. I take a moment to calm myself before continuing. "How was I supposed to come to you both when you both pretty much accused me of getting pregnant so I could get paid for the rest of my life?" When neither of them answers I scoff, pussies. "Exactly, so I did what I thought was best. I mean, you both did say I would never be a good mother to her, thanks to me being a fucking depressed piece of shit from losing my best friend. I believed you assholes. The family she showed me looked amazing and had a great home and well-paying jobs, so I thought she would be better off with them. It wasn't until after I gave birth to her..." I start to get choked up at the memories of her. I push those away and focus on the here and now. "Forty-eight hours later, I signed the papers. Nathan signed his name as her father. The doctors never questioned it, he was there for every scan, every doctor's appointment and her birth."

"He was there?"

"Yes, Crue, Nate was there with me." Hurt clouds their faces but fuck them, they did me wrong! "The moment I saw Jackson walk in with the woman from the adoption agency I knew something was wrong. I tried to back out but it was too late, I had signed away my rights. Ever since I got out of the hospital I have been working every angle I can to get the information I needed on Adalyn."

"Why the fuck were you with Jackson the night we saw you?" Try as he might, I can still hear the jealousy in Sanit's voice.

"I was with him so I could try cloning the bastard's phone. Think of me what you will, but I would never fucking betray Crue like that." I hear the conviction in my own voice. I turn to Crue needing him to see the truth in my eyes and hear it in my words. "You may hate me and we may have issues right now but I would *never* betray you like that." He searches my eyes for a minute before giving me a curt nod. I look down and see the bottles half full. I turn the pump off and start the process of unscrewing and capping the bottles before ridding myself of the contraption, I keep my back to them as I get dressed. I can feel their eyes on me the entire time and fight the shiver that wants to break free. I shove everything into my bag after dressing and throw it over my shoulder, I'm about to reach for the four bottles when Saint's words stop me.

"Did you get his phone?"

I shake my head as I answer. "No, the bastard took off after dropping me at the club. I had to surprise him at his office to clone it and that was when I found out who really adopted Adalyn."

"What else did you find?" Crue pushes.

"He sells children to the families that have been rejected by the agency and gets paid a shit load for it. I don't know how he or Devon knew about Adalyn, I never told anyone aside from you both and our friends."

"The pictures on your phone, are they the only ones you have?" I smile sadly at Saint and nod.

"I only got two days with her before they took her from me." Crue's gaze hardens.

"Still more than we fucking got with her," he snaps.

"Don't fucking come at me for this shit, I did what I thought was best for her!"

"Do me a favor, rub your hand between your legs and take a whiff of that shit because your ass has bigger fish to fry." I balk at Crue, how fucking dare he.

"Fuck you both, neither of you were there——"

"And who's fucking fault is that?" Saint shouts. "You're here to help bring her home, the moment we get back to CHU we'll pay whatever you want so you can get the fuck out of ours and Adalyn's lives for good!"

"Go fuck yourselves. You stand there thinking you are holier than thou, yet you both are the fucking reason I chose adoption. You blame me for leaving, but neither of you gave me a fucking reason to stay. I made a selfless choice because I thought it was best for her."

I stand here brimming with anger as they both turn and leave, then stand here alone and utterly devastated by Saint's harsh words. Can neither of them see that I thought I was doing the right thing? I have been trying to get her back since the moment Jackson took her from me. I fucked up, I know that, but I am trying every fucking thing I can to get our girl back. Now I fear that getting her back won't be the end of this nightmare.

I can feel it now, Crue and Saint are going to make me rue the day I left them and keep our girl a secret.

CHAPTER ELEVEN

Crue

Saint and I never spoke to Katie the entire flight after we left her in the bathroom. Halfway through the flight, Nathan came up to check on her and it took everything in my power not to snap his neck when she grabbed her bag and led him to the bathroom to express again. I could see Saint was barely able to contain himself as well. I fucking hate Nathan. What he did is unforgivable! That cunt fucked with my family and you don't get away with that shit.

The moment the plane touched down in Auckland, we had to rush to our connecting flight to Queenstown. When we finally landed there, I felt like I could breathe easier. I don't recommend traveling thirteen hours straight and then hopping on another flight for an extra two hours. My ass is fucking numb, I stink, I need sleep and I need something fucking good to eat! The seven of us went straight to the rental car place and got the keys for the two cars, then headed straight to the hotel to get some shut eye. It may only be noon here but fuck me, I couldn't sleep a wink on either flight with her so close to me.

Katie and Leah ride with us while Darius and Beck travel with the cunt. Beck and I check us all in and grab the key cards from the receptionist. Beck hands Darius his card and then grabs his shit. I motion for Saint to follow me, then turn ready to hit the elevators until she speaks.

"Where do we sleep?" I look over my shoulder at her and growl out,

"Your ass is with us, the cunt stays with Beck." Her eyes widen, I don't stick around to hear her bullshit reply.

She may be pissed the fuck off at us but she follows us in the elevator nonetheless. The moment we step into the room, she throws her case on one of the double beds, grabs some clothes, and then storms into the bathroom, slamming the door closed behind herself. Saint falls face first onto the other bed and moans while I place my shit on the other side of the room near the window. The view is fucking beautiful, mountains as far as the eye can see. The grass and trees are so green here, the people are so bloody nice as well and smile at you for nothing.

"If she doesn't hurry the fuck up in there, you're going to be stuck sleeping next to my dirty ass because I can't keep my eyes open any longer."

Snorting, I turn away from the window and slap his ass. He shrieks like a fucking girl and lurches up the bed, rolling to his back and glaring down at me. "Your ass is always dirty."

A devilish glint enters his eyes as he rests his arms behind his head and smirks at me. "Coming from the guy who had my cum dripping out of his ass?" My snarky reply is cut off by the sound of a gasp coming from the left. We both turn our heads to see Katie standing there in a shirt that looks awfully familiar.

"Is that my Slipknot shirt?" She ignores my question as she looks between the both of us.

"You two slept together... without... me?" It shocks me more that I don't hear hurt in her tone but happiness.

"What's it to you if we did?" Saint snaps.

She shrugs her shoulders and shakes her head. "Nothing. I'm just glad you both finally expressed how you really felt for each other." She shoves her clothes in her case and I'm stuck here staring at her like she's a strange being.

"What the fuck is that supposed to mean?" I finally ask as she lifts her leg and perches it on the edge of the bed and then proceeds to rub cream all over her calf and works her way to her thigh, my shirt rides up and I can just make out the pink of her panties that peeks out from under her shirt.

"Crue, I've known from the start that the both of you had a *thing*. I was just shocked it took you guys this long to finally admit that you love each other," she says with a shrug like it's not a big deal.

"I'm too tired for this shit," Saint grits out as he climbs off the bed and heads for the shower, leaving the door open. It takes a fuck load of effort for me to tear my gaze off Katie when she reaches the top of her thigh. I stare out the window and try to focus on anything else but what she's doing behind me. Her approval or acceptance shouldn't mean shit to me, I don't need her blessing to love Saint. I mean, I do love him but I guess just not in the way I originally thought I did. He and I worked so well because *she* was there. She kept us together and made the both of us feel okay exploring each other through her.

"The fuck." At the sound of Saint's outburst, I spin around, to see him standing in the bathroom doorway with a towel around his waist. I follow his line of sight and my own eyes widen, Katie sits on the bed in nothing but her pink panties with the pump thing hooked up to her tits again.

"What? I told you I have to do this every couple hours." She sounds exasperated and miffed.

"Put some fucking clothes on," he grits out.

She rolls her eyes. "Please, it's not like you haven't seen it all before."

Saint throws his hands in the air. "That's exactly the fucking point." She scrunches her face in confusion.

"Uh, that makes zero sense." Saint shoots me a look imploring me to help him out here.

"He means cover the fuck up or get the fuck on your knees. We can all stand here and deny it as much as we want but the truth is, the fucking sight of you gets our cocks hard." Her jaw unhinges. The fact she is shocked by my comment is comical, she knows I don't fucking mince words when it comes to her or Saint. I say it how it is.

"I-I can't, I have to pump—" She doesn't get a chance to finish her sentence, Saint leaps onto her bed, grips the back of her neck, pulling her closer so he can kiss her. The sight of them getting lost in each other has my cock twitching in my pants. Saint begins to paw at the pump thing to get it off her but she hisses in pain. Breaking the kiss, she begins to unstrap the thing and places it to the side before throwing herself at Saint again. Saint forces her flat on her back and then nestles himself between her legs. I slowly close the space between us and stand at the edge of the bed as he slowly trails open mouthed kisses down her exposed throat. When he reaches her tits he doesn't suck, instead, he darts his tongue out and flicks it across her enlarged peaks, her back arches off the bed as a cry tears from her throat.

"You like that, Katie baby?" I ask as I grip her hair and turn her gaze to me, her eyes wild and filled with need.

"Y-yes," she moans as Saint slowly licks a trail down her body. Fuck, the moment he grips her panties and peels them down her legs, I'm fucking done. I rip my shirt off and rid myself of my pants and boxers.

"Get on your hands and knees," I growl. She does as I demand. I slip onto the bed and rest against the headboard. she licks her lips at the sight of my hard cock.

"Suck him while I eat this pussy, Katie baby." Her only

response is to moan. The moment her dainty little hand grips the base of my dick I jerk in her hold.

"Fuck, Saint," she cries out when he begins to eat her greedy little pussy. Wrapping her hair around my fist, I force her mouth down onto my cock. Shit, the feeling of her tight wet mouth on me has a primal groan pulling free.

"Hollow your cheeks, baby." She does as I say and Jesus Christ, it feels fucking amazing. The moment she cups my balls and moans around my dick, I moan so fucking loud.

"Fuck that's hot." I cut a glance to Saint to see him watching Katie bob up and down on my cock like a porn star. "Don't fucking cum, Crue." I grit my teeth and watch as he drops his towel and lines himself up with her entrance. I know the moment he begins to push inside her, she tenses and the vibrations from the moans coming out of her send shockwaves up my spine. "Fuck, you fit me so good, baby," Saint grits out the moment he's balls deep inside her.

"Hmmm," comes from her as Saint begins to move. The moment he thrust hard inside her, she rips her mouth off my cock and screams out. Leaning forward I grip her chin and hold her in place never allowing her gaze to waiver from mine. Saint fucks her hard and fuck me, it's the hottest sight I have ever seen —watching her eyes morph into a blissed-out state the harder he continues to fuck her. "I'm coming, Saint, don't fucking stop!"

Before she can scream any louder, I force her mouth back to my cock and groan. "Saint, I'm not gonna last much longer," I growl.

"Ahhhhh," Katie screams out around me as she comes, shudders rolling through her entire body and fuck, it's sexy to watch. I feel my balls begin to tighten as she begins to deep throat me.

"Yeah, baby, like that." I see the strain on Saint's face and know he's close, I start thrusting into her mouth chasing my own release. Within a minute, Saint and I are both roaring out our release with her name on both our lips. I hold her head in place until she swallows every fucking drop of my cum, call me sick or whatever but I love knowing that I'm inside her at the same time Saint is.

I sit in the chair next to the desk in the room and stare at Katie's sleeping form. Saint is perched on the edge of the desk beside me. She never said a word to us after we fucked. She climbed off the bed, took another shower, then crawled into bed and fell asleep.

"Did you see her tattoo?" Saint whispers.

"Yeah."

"No, I mean did you actually look at it, Crue?" Frowning I turn and look up at him with a brow raised prompting him to continue. "The tattoo has *us* in it." I reel back shaking my head.

"Bullshit."

"Dude, the thing runs down half the side of her body, and onto one of her ass cheeks, believe me, I got a good look at her ass today." The fucker sounds smug so I shove him.

"Whatever dick."

"Crue, I'm serious."

I run a hand through my hair and nod. "I know, but that changes nothing. She can tattoo my name on her pussy but it still—-"

"'Your name is on her ass." I laugh expecting him to laugh along with me, except he doesn't, and my eyes widen.

"Wait, you're fucking serious?" He just nods. Fuck this. I'm on my feet in the next second and ripping the covers off her before straddling the back of her thighs. She wakes, screaming in fright, but I ignore her screams and use the grip I have on her hair to shove her face into the pillow to mute her while I use my other hand to lift her shirt.

CHAPTER TWELVE

Katie

I try to buck my hips to throw his heavy ass off but he doesn't budge. "Why the fuck do you have our names tattooed on your ass?" Crue snarls. I try to turn my head but the grip he has on my neck keeps me in place.

"She can't answer with her face stuffed in the pillow, bro," Saint says.

"Oh," is all Crue says before he releases me. I try to roll over but he still won't get the fuck off my legs.

"Move!" Crue's eyes harden as he stares at me. "I said move, Crue." I enforce as much authority as I can into my tone. The bastard just pins me with a bored look and crosses his arms over his chest.

"Answer his question," Saint interjects. I flick my gaze to him and scowl at the bastard.

"I got them as a reminder," I finally admit after a moment. There's a football field, football and each of their playing numbers as well as their names tattooed on my ass.

"Why?"

"Because I wanted to, Saint. It's my body to do with as I please." The smug prick crosses his arms over his chest and quirks a brow.

"Your body, huh?" The heat in his words has me trying to clench my thighs together but thanks to Crue, that's not happening.

"She was born on December first," he quietly whispers from behind me. He pushes my shirt up farther and inspects the tattoo, before I know it Saint is yanking my shirt off me and forcing me flat on the mattress so they can further inspect the ink themselves. The room is bathed in silence for a long while. I begin to drift back to sleep until I feel Crue's fingertips trailing down my arm as he looks over every inch of my tattoo. "It's a mural," he whispers.

"What?"

Crue ignores Saint as he asks, "Why would you get a tattoo dedicated to us?" A whoosh of air escapes me as I melt farther into the mattress, I knew Crue would be the one to figure it out. Between him and Saint, he is the more attentive one. He pays closer attention to my moods, my reactions and just my entire being really. Saint is the more hands-on forceful one. He can't read a mood to save his life, he doesn't do boundaries or space, he needs everything spelled out for him. They are the perfect Yin and Yang. "Answer me, Katie."

Tears begin to build behind my eyes as I explain, "After Adalyn was taken from me, I needed something of her with me always. What better way to carry my daughter with me then to ink my body with the story of how she came to be."

"Wait, I don't follow."

I flick my gaze to Saint and spell it out for him. "The start of Adalyn's journey begins with you and Crue." I point blindly behind me at my ass and then to my side. "The cabin, the house at CHU, Christmas, losing Cody, us breaking up, me leaving, finding out she still lived inside me and the day my life changed forever." All of that is marked in ink on my skin, only the three of us would be able to tell what each of these places means that are immortalized on my skin. I have a portrait of Adalyn on the side of my shoulder, it's the first photo I took of her.

"You literally branded us into your skin… for life."

I peer over my shoulder at Crue and shrug. "There is nothing about the time I've spent with you both that I will ever regret, well, except for *that night*," I answer honestly, his eyes drill into me trying to search for a sign of deceit. He won't find it.

"Did you… did you find out…" Crue lets his sentence trail off, I know what he's asking me.

"No. It didn't matter to me which of you created her, for me you're both her fathers no matter what a test says." They both relax at my words. Crue slowly slips off me and sits on the edge of the bed near where Saint stands. I sit up and tuck my legs under myself.

"I want to forgive you, Katie, I really do." My breath lodges in my throat at Crue's words. "I don't know how I can though. You gave our baby away to a monster." I bite my lip to try tamper my anger at his accusation but I fail.

"I had no fucking idea he was the one who adopted her. Like I said, I chose a family to adopt her. It wasn't until that fucking asshole Jackson showed up that I knew something was off."

"I have to know." I dart my gaze to Saint who is staring at the floor like this is hard for him to say. I want to reach out and touch him to try to ease his worries but I can't. I lost that right. "Why did you run?" He peeks up at me through his lashes and the broken look in his eyes spears me right in the chest.

"I was scared," I answer honestly. "Neither of you have ever raised your voice or shown me the angry asshole sides of you that others see, except the night you found the test. You both accused me of getting pregnant on purpose, when I never planned to have kids. I knew neither of you wanted children, I respected that."

"Then why the fuck did you hide it from us?" Crue demands.

"I found out a couple weeks before Cody passed, I was planning on telling you both but then you were so caught up in helping Beck find Val's stalker and everything with Corvin that I didn't want to add to your stress. I wanted to tell you both so many times but then… I just couldn't. I know I should have been honest and I am sorry. I was fucking depressed and spiraling over everything that happened. I just didn't know how to tell you both about the baby without causing more pain."

They both remain silent for a while and I begin to worry that they will leave me again. "I'm sorry your family kicked you out." I recoil in shock at Saint's words. "You could have gotten rid of her but you didn't. Yes, we did act like fucking assholes and shouldn't have said what we did to you. You never blamed our daughter for how we behaved and the things we fucking said were disgusting…" Saint sighs and runs a hand through his hair in frustration. "Thank you, Katie."

Now the tears trail down my cheeks without consent, a sob tears from me. Within a second Saint is on the bed and wrapping his arms around me and holding me close as I break down. I've never let myself cry like this. I knew if I did, I wouldn't have anyone there to pick the pieces of me up and put me back together but now, with the two men I love most in this world, I know I can because they will always put my pieces back together. Saint holds me until I eventually cry myself back to sleep.

I jolt awake at the sound of a phone ringing. I open my eyes and cringe, I can feel how puffy they are from crying. I look around and see I'm still in Saint's lap with his arms wrapped around me, Crue is lying next to us with his hand on my thigh. My heart soars, we have so much to sort out between us but still, when I needed them most, they pulled through and held me through the pain. The phone rings again. I frown when I realize it's coming from Crue's pocket. I carefully reach for it trying not to wake him. When I see it's Darius calling I answer it.

"Hello?"

"Uh, Katie?"

"Yeah, it's me, Darius," I whisper.

He sighs and chuckles nervously. "Thank fuck, that would have been awkward if it was some random—"

"Can I help you?" I cut in before he can finish that fucking stupid-ass sentence. He clears his throat before continuing.

"It's after nine now. I was checking if the goon squad still wanted to do recon." I'm about to tell him that they are both asleep when I feel Saint place a kiss on the top of my head. I look to Crue to find his eyes wide open and staring directly at me. He smiles and holds his hand out for his phone. I hand it over without complaint and snuggle into Saint.

"What up?" Crue says. "Yeah, give us ten then we'll meet you in the lobby," he says before ending the call and pocketing his phone again.

"Who was that?" Saint asks as he runs his fingers through my hair.

"D, we leave in ten to scope out Devon's place before we hit him tomorrow." At the mention of his father Saint tenses and his fingers still in my hair.

"Yeah, okay," he forces out. I shoot look at Crue, conveying without words that Saint isn't ready for this.

"You want to stay here with Katie while I go?" Crue offers, though he and I both know Saint won't let him go on his own, they do everything together.

"Nah, my man, let's do this." Before either of them can move off the bed, I lean down and place a kiss on Crue's lips then I do the same to Saint. They both sit there stunned and looking slightly nervous.

"Don't say anything okay, I just want you both to know

that I'm sorry. I know I fucked up and I own that shit. We have hurt each other and need to work everything out. I want this to work with you two because I can't fucking live without either of you, I'm a shell without you both. I love you both so much." Their eyes widen at my declaration. "I don't expect you to say it back——"

"I love you too." My eyes widen at Crue's admission.

"You know, I fucking love you both." I turn to Saint shocked. "We got shit to sort but right now, all I care about is getting our daughter back and getting the fuck home, then we can work out whatever the fuck we need to."

Saint and Crue didn't even argue when I told them I was coming. I sit in the middle of them in the back seat as Beck drives while Darius rides shotgun. I knew there was no way that they would allow Nathan to come. They have stated to forgive me, but I have no doubt it will take longer for them to extend the same courtesy to my friend. I expected Devon to live in an apartment or something lavish but the cottage style home the guys point out isn't what I had expected at all. It looks like the type of place where happy families spend their holidays, a house filled with love if you will.

Beck parks a mile down the road so we don't alert Devon. Before they can exit the car, I speak. "Hang on, let me check if he has a security system." Four sets of gazes are on me. I ignore them as I reach into my backpack and pull out my laptop. None of them question me as I do my thing, I've proven myself to them time and again with how good I am at hacking and digging up dirt on people. I mean, I was the one who managed to find out Jackson's hidden talents of cross dressing and stripping at the club two towns over. "Shit."

"What?" Darius asks, I look up from my screen as I say.

"I hacked his computer, the guy doesn't change passwords so it was easy. He has motion sensor security and the house is fitted with a top of the line alarm system monitored by a security agency nearby."

"Can you disarm it?" Crue asks. I tap away on my keyboard trying to disarm it but then I see the embedded code and stop.

"No, if I keep hacking into the system it will alert the company as soon as I deactivate it." I slump back into my seat feeling defeated.

"What do we do now?" Beck asks. No one answers for a while. We're so close, she is literally mere feet away, and we can't even get to her!

CHAPTER THIRTEEN

I know what I have to do, Crue is going to go crazy but I have to do this, she needs me and I won't leave her.

"Fuck all of you!" I roar as I push my door open and leap out of the car. I don't hang around, I head for my father's house.

"Saint!" I hear Crue shout but I don't stop, then the sound of their footfalls chasing me can be heard. I harden my features and prepare myself for what I'm about to do. Crue grips my arm and rips me around, but before he can blink, my fist strikes out and clips across his jaw. He lands on his ass as Beck and Darius rush toward me, but I back up a couple of steps. Katie stands behind them with wide eyes. "What the fuck?" he yells.

I pin him with a cold emotionless look. "Did you seriously think I would ever raise my daughter with the likes of you?" Hurt clouds his features but I push on. "The last thing I need is for her to be around someone like you who can't decide what the fuck they want."

"Saint, that's enough!" I snap my angry scowl to Katie.

"You don't get to fucking speak, you're just as bad as him. Neither of your families wanted you."

"Shut the fuck up, Saint."

"Fuck you, Darius!" I bite out. Out of the corner of my eye I see a light flick on in the house and know without a doubt his security system caught everything I just said. "Get the fuck out of here, I'm done with all you fuckers." I turn on my heel and head for the cottage, my chest aching with pain.

"Don't you dare fucking do this. I know you and this isn't going to work you asshole, I'm right here and I won't let you do this to us." I stop but keep my back to him, if I turn around now and Crue sees the look in my eyes he'll know. "I love you, Saint. I'm here and I'm begging you... Please don't fucking do this." The broken tone of his voice kills me, but I can't. This is the only way.

"I never loved you or her, go home, Crue, and take your bitch with you because I'm done with you both. It was fun while it lasted but now I'm over it. I already told you once, I'll never fuck you again, you were a bet, Crue, nothing more." The strangled sob that comes from Katie nearly has me crumbling to my knees, but I hold strong.

"You son of a bitch, don't you fucking dare do this to him." I ignore Katie as I force my feet to move. I feel their gazes on me the whole way until I disappear around the corner of the driveway and just like I knew he would be, my father stands in the open doorway of his house. Devon Morgan, the star of all my nightmares and the sole reason I never wanted children. A sinister smile stretches across his weathered face, his salt and pepper hair in disarray, but looking into his eyes, I see my own.

"The prodigal son returns." The sound of his voice sends a shiver down my spine. I take a deep breath and remind myself he can't hurt me anymore. I'm not the same eight-year-old boy he used to smack around for inheriting my mother's estate and not him.

"Well, it appears you have something that belongs to me and I want her back." I hear a car drive off behind me and my heart sinks. Crue is going to hate me and so is Katie. I just threw their biggest insecurities back in their faces, the things I said to my best friend is unforgivable.

He crosses his arms over his chest and hardens his stare. "*My* daughter is fast asleep."

I grind my teeth so fucking hard they begin to ache. "Well, I would love to see her and you know, discuss the wineries and vineyards." He can try as he might but I see the fucking twinkle in his eyes at the mention of getting what he's always wanted. "I turn twenty-one in two months, pops," I taunt.

He smirks. "I already won, boy, you took over the company," he says smugly but now it's my turn to smirk.

"Nah." His falls slightly. "You see I set it up in a trust with BCD'S so what that means is I don't technically own it, so that means at this point in time no one gets the wineries or Vineyards."

"You fucking idiot, you're throwing away millions a month," he seethes.

"Invite me in so I can meet *my* daughter, and then we'll talk."

He eyes me skeptically for a moment. "How did you find out about her?"

I pin him with a board look. "Jackson Rathborne wasn't the smartest choice. You don't think I've had eyes on him for years?"

His eyes narrow. "I won't allow your filth near her, you come back you best be done with that sissy boy." Anger burns through my veins, making me shove my hands into my pockets so he can't them clenched into fists at the way he speaks about Crue.

"Let me break it down for you, old man. My cock is still covered with the come of the bitch I was fucking back at the hotel, want a whiff?" His face scrunched in disgust.

"You try anything, Saint, and I'll have your ass arrested and my company back from you within a day, got it?" I nod stiffly, he isn't lying. The fucking cunt would love to see me rotting behind bars so he has an excuse as to why I can't run the company and he can inherit my mother's fortune without me.

"You have my word, I just want to meet my daughter."

⚜

I sit here in the rocking chair next to the window with her wrapped in my arms. She's so tiny. She's perfect. The moment he led me to her room and unlocked the door, I shoved his ass aside and went straight to her. I have no idea what the fuck I'm doing but she doesn't seem to mind me just holding her— she's real and she's mine. I've been sitting here for hours, the sun is cresting the horizon now. I've seen at least half a dozen armed men walk past the open doorway and I know without a doubt I made the right decision. Devon would have used my daughter against me if we had of snuck in.

"Excuse me." I snap my gaze to the doorway and tighten my hold slightly on my daughter as I look over at the old woman who stands there wearing… Fuck's sake, she's dressed in an actual maid's uniform. "It's time for her bottle and bottom change." She takes one step toward me and that's when I snap.

"I'll do it. Bring me the shit and I'll do it myself." She frowns and pinches her lips to the side, but nods and leaves to get me what I want. I stare back down at my girl and smile, her little eyes are open and she yawns up at me. "Good morning, beautiful princess." She starts to stretch in my hold and I laugh, this is the first time she has woken up since I got here. "I'm your daddy," I whisper past the lump in my throat. Tears cloud my vision as she smiles up at me. She has Katie's eyes. She's fucking perfect. "I'm going to make sure you never wonder your worth or if you're loved because, princess, you already own my whole heart."

"Here you go." The maid returns with a bottle which she hands me. I go to give her the bottle the maid stops me. "You need to cradle her against your chest and tilt her slightly so she isn't lying flat." I do as she says and try again but my girl doesn't seem to like the bottle. "Oh dear." I cut my gaze to her.

"What?"

She frowns as she looks down at my girl. "Mr. Morgan has tried to transition her onto formula but she doesn't seem to be taking to it well." Anger soars through me, that fucking cunt.

"I'll get her to drink her milk," I grit out. The maid stays until Adalyn finally latches onto the bottle. She points out where the diapers and wipes are before she leaves. She has a really fucking cool accent. She had no idea what the hell I was saying when I asked for the Pampers, I've learned they are called *nappies* here in New Zealand. I pull my phone and ignore the calls and texts from the others as I YouTube how to change a baby. This is a fucking first for me so I want to make sure I do it right. After burping and changing my girl's bum I return to the rocking chair and hold her against my chest as I rock us back and forth. The moment my phone vibrates in my pocket I sigh. I pull it out careful not to wake my baby, it's Beckett.

Fuck it. "What do you want, Beck?" I hiss quietly.

"Don't you dare hang up." I tense at the sound of Crue's voice, a minute of silence passes before he finally speaks. "I know you can't talk because he'll have that place bugged. I'm fucking livid, Saint, I'm going to fucking beat the shit out of you for this stunt." I take a shuddering breath.

"Get to the point," I say angrily.

"Fake being angry all you want, dick face, you may have Darius and Beckett convinced you're a worthless piece of shit but not me and Katie. I know why you did it..."

"Stop—"

"No. You fucking listen to me, asshole. I had to take everything you threw at me so you can—-"

"Don't call again," I grit out just as my girl begins to cry and I end the call. I rock her back and forth and tap her little bottom as I look around and whisper low enough for only her to hear. "Your other daddy is angry with me, soon you will get to meet him and your mommy."

"Saint." I dart my gaze to the doorway to see my father standing there, he looks to Adalyn and the moment I see his lip curl in disgust I tighten my hold on my daughter. "Get rid of her and meet me in the living room."

"She stays with me," I grit out. His eyes narrow in warning but I won't budge. I don't trust this cunt not to hurt her to get at me.

"Bring it then." Son of a bitch, I'm going to enjoy watching this fucker get torn down a peg or ten when I'm through with him. I follow after him, not missing the guards he has stationed around the house. Paranoid motherfucker. I sit in the chair furthest away from him. He drops a folder on the coffee table in the middle of the room, making a loud smacking noise that has Adalyn screaming in fright. I'm on my feet and rocking her and trying to soothe her. "Shut it up." I pin him with a hard look.

"You can come at me any time you like, but you don't ever come for my fucking daughter, Devon. I'll burn the fucking wineries if you push me on this. Sign her over to me and I'll give you what you want."

"Nice try, you take my company out of your trust and list me as your partner, then when you turn twenty-one you state that I take over everything and you walk away with nothing."

"Done." His eyes narrow.

"You try anything—-"

"I don't fucking need it Devon, keep your pathetic company, take mom's shit, I don't care. I just want my daughter."

"Yeah, that's not gonna work for me." Dread starts to pool inside me. "You don't get her until after the court case."

"What case?"

His eyes narrow. "I have to attend court next week. Your fucking lawyer found me. You come to court with me and claim you want full custody and as my son and her legal guardian, the court has no choice but to drop the case."

"Why?"

"It's going to take at least three weeks to get this shit with the vineyards and wineries sorted, so I can't let my bargaining chip go now, can I?"

"How did you even know about her?" He rolls his eyes.

"You should really keep a closer eye on your surroundings son. I've had a tail on you, it's mother and the sissy boy since your little takeover. It was too fucking easy to get Jackson to help, he hates the sissy as much as I do and was all too willing to help me." Anger like I have never felt courses through my veins. "I knew the bitch would come to you eventually and sure enough, here you are, ready to give me what I want all because of a bastard."

I knew it. Devon saw his golden opportunity to get what he has always wanted the moment Katie gave Adalyn up for adoption. He never cared about my daughter, she was just a pawn to be used to lure me out so I would give him what he has always wanted. I'll play along for now, but as soon as I get a second, I need to call Troy and get the ball rolling because this cock sucker is going down for thinking he could take my baby from me without repercussions. He is the reason I never wanted children. I grew up feeling unlovable because of him. Not once in my life has my father ever told me he was proud of me or that he even loved me.

"Sign the papers, boy," he demands.

"Not until you sign her over to me."

The moment six of his guards enter the room I know what's coming. Devon smirks wickedly. I spy the maid out of the corner of my eye, hovering in the doorway. Taking a deep breath, I place a kiss on my girl's forehead and nod for her to come take her. The moment Adalyn is out of the room I turn back to Devon and crack my neck side to side.

"Let's get this beating over with shall we?"

"It doesn't have to be this way, you're a star now, boy. You really want pictures of you snapped and posted online covered in bruises?"

"We gonna keep playing with our dicks or get this shit over with, because I'm not signing anything, motherfucker."

His eyes darken as his upper lip pulls back in a snarl. "Teach him a lesson," he says to his bitch boys before they come at me. I'm man enough to admit I know I don't stand a chance against six guys. This beating is going to hurt like a bitch but at least it's just me receiving it. I have no doubt if Crue had come with me, Devon would have forced me to watch him get his ass beat and that is something I could never do.

CHAPTER FOURTEEN

Katie

It's been two days since Saint left us. Crue and I know he didn't mean anything he said. I managed to hack into the cameras that surround the property and sure enough everything he said was caught on tape just like he knew it would be. Hurting me and Crue was his way of showing his father that we meant nothing to him. As crazy as it sounds, I love him more for doing what he did to ensure our daughter was safe.

"We have to fly back to the States, we don't have a choice," Darius says from across the lunch table we're sitting at.

"The court case," I breathe out. Crue places his hand atop my thigh under the table offering his silent support. He and I have clung to each other since Saint left.

"Do you think he will even attend?" Nathan asks cautiously from my other side. Crue grows tense beside me but remains silent. He still can't look at Nathan or even speak to him, and that fucking hurts because Nate was only doing what I asked of him.

"He's been subpoenaed, he has no choice." Beck tacks on,

"But, I agree, I need to get the fuck home because my son misses me. If we all agree, I'll book flights for tomorrow."

"Wait, what about Saint?" Leah asks.

Darius rubs the back of his neck and looks slightly sheepish as he says, "Uh, I'm gonna need his shit and passport. He's asked me to drop it at the gate of his dad's." He's barely finished speaking before Crue is shoving back from the table and storming off toward the elevators that will take him to our room. I shoot the others a sad smile before I follow after my man, this whole situation is fucking hard for him. Saint and Crue are a pair, without the other they are lost. I see it in his eyes, Crue has no idea how to function without Saint. He holds the lift doors open for me, and the second they close, he's on me. He grips my waist and lifts me. I wrap my arms and legs around him, holding on for dear life as his tongue forces it's way past my lips. He grinds against me and I gasp when I feel how hard he is for me. Breaking the kiss, he looks over at the keypad and hits the emergency stop.

"Crue!"

"Shut up, Katie. I need to fuck you now so either deal with that or get the fuck on your knees." The look in his blue eyes shows me everything. He needs this so he can feel a connection between him and I. This will be the first time I have ever slept with just one of them.

"Take whatever you need from me." My words are his undoing. He reaches between us and forces my panties to the side, slipping a finger inside me.

"Fuck, you're soaked." I throw my head and cry out the moment he plunges two fingers inside my greedy cunt. "You gonna be a good girl and take my cock, Katie baby?"

"Yes, I need you inside me now, Crue." He makes quick work of freeing his cock from the confines of his jeans, then in one swift move he's slamming inside me. We both cry out at the feeling of being joined in the best fucking way possible.

"Hold on to me, baby." I do as he says and tighten my arms and legs around him. He fucks me hard. God, he isn't holding back and I fucking love it. "I love you, Katie, I can't." *Thrust.* "Lose." *Thrust.* "You." *Thrust.* "Too."

Cupping his face between my hands, I smash my lips against his for a minute until I break it with a cry. "I fucking love you too. I'm here Crue, always. Now make me come." My wish is answered as he thrusts so hard inside me, I come screaming his name. He pulls out and shoves me to my knees. He reaches down and rips the front of my dress, exposing my tits before pumping himself.

"Katie," he roars as jets of cum land on my exposed chest and chin. "Fuck." he grits out as he stumbles back a step and stares down at me covered in his cum, with a possessive smile on his beautiful face. "You're mine. Anyone who tries to take you from me will end up in the hole next to Val's father." I gasp. He kneels down in front of me, grips my chin and then uses his thumb to smear his cum over my lips. "Let's get the fuck out of here so we can go home, get our boy and finally bring our daughter home." He has no fucking idea how much his words have hope spurring to life inside me.

Crue and I are nearly finished packing our bags when a knock sounds at the door. Crue shoots me a wink from the other side of the bed before going to answer it, expecting it to be Darius coming to collect Saint's things. Crue and I both decided that it was best if we didn't accompany D and Beck to drop his things off as neither of us would have been able to leave there without him and our daughter.

"Who the hell are you?" I drop the shirt I was folding and rush over to Crue to find an elderly lady standing there, looking terrified.

"My name is Roimata and I'm your daughters nanny. May I come in?" We stand here shocked for a second, unmoving. I snap out of it quicker than Crue.

"Of course, please come in Roi—Sorry, I don't know how to say your name," I say, slightly embarrassed. She waves me off with a warm smile and enters the room. Crue closes the door as we all stand here awkwardly for a moment until Crue speaks.

"Why are you here?" Her shoulders bunch.

"I shouldn't be here but Saint begged me. I can't stay long. Mr. Morgan has eyes everywhere and if I'm caught—"

I cut off her panicked rambling. "We won't say a word, please just tell us if he's okay?"

She flinches and my stomach drops. Crue wraps his arm around my shoulders and draws me into his side. "He's… Okay."

"Don't lie to me," Crue snarls. Her shoulders droop and a sad look takes over her features.

"He was beaten." I gasp and tears spring to my eyes instantly. Crue's hold on me tightens.

"Why?" Crue grits out.

"He refused to sign the papers. I don't know all the details but he asked me to come here and tell you they will be there for the court case but you need to be ready."

"Ready for what?" I choke out.

"He said to tell you, he loves her no matter what and will do whatever he has to so she can come home. I'm sorry but that's all I know. I have to go." We don't stop her as she leaves. My mind is reeling and I don't know how to process what she has said. All I can focus on is the fact that he will be at court.

"Whatever he has planned must be something big if he took such a huge risk sending her here." I pull back and stare up at Crue, my stomach in knots with worry.

"Why did he hurt him?" Crue's eyes soften.

"Devon hates that Saint isn't under his control anymore. He's always hated Saint because his mother left him everything. Devon is smart, Katie. He'll have a plan in place, so we just have to make sure that we are ready for whatever he has planned and don't fuck it up."

"He can't get away with hurting him," I snarl. Crue cups my face between his hands and bends so we are eye to eye.

"He won't get away with any of this, nor will Jackson. We'll take all the fuckers down, and then we will all be fucking free of this shit and finally able to live our lives."

An hour or so later, Darius comes by to collect Saint's things. I made sure to pack all the breast milk I had stored in the fridge into his bag. If he chooses to dump it, then fine, but I really hope he doesn't. The thought of her drinking my milk makes me feel closer to my baby while I can't physically be there.

"Look, I know this whole thing is fucked but if it helps, I think he has a plan." Crue and I share a loaded look before turning back to face Darius.

"What do you mean?" I ask.

"Troy has gone radio silent and isn't answering any of mine, Becks or Corvin's calls, so we think Saint is up to something."

"He's got something up his sleeve for the court case," Crue mutters.

"Yeah, man, I think he has something in the works," he says before grabbing Saint's things and leaving Crue and I alone in our room. Time passes by slowly as we sit here silently and get lost in our thoughts. What if he's really hurt and needs help? All these horrible scenes are flashing through my mind and I don't realize I'm crying until Crue reaches over and swipes the tears from my cheeks.

"He's strong." I sniff and nod. He clasps my hands in his and gives them a gentle squeeze. "Whatever he has planned, we'll back him. Saint is cunning, he's also fucking smart. Contrary to what everyone believes, he isn't stupid. He knew what he was doing the other night, it was the only way Devon would let him in. I have a feeling that he got his ass beat because he wouldn't sign over the company and his inheritance to his father."

"I thought with him taking over Devon's company he already got it?"

Crue shakes his head. "I'm gonna tell you something that no one else knows, not even the guys." The grave tone of his voice has me sitting up straighter and paying closer attention.

"I swear, I won't tell a soul."

"Saint doesn't own Morgan Tech IT." I scrunch my face in confusion, trying to read between the lines of what he's saying.

"I don't understand, he did the hostile takeover and pushed his father out."

Crue nods. "Yes. He put the company in a trust so that technically he doesn't run it. As long as he doesn't run it or own it as such, Devon can't touch his inheritance. He never took over the company and ran it once Devon was out. He changed the name and shut down all the illegal shit his dad was doing, but he left it to be run by the board until after he turned twenty-one."

"Crue, I'm not following," I say honestly.

"If Saint took over the company now, before he turned twenty-one, Devon would get half of everything that was left to Saint by his mother. He needs to wait till after he turns twenty-one to claim the company as the owner, then be able to run it as he sees fit."

I'm missing something here, I see it in his eyes. Crue would never betray Saint by telling me his secrets, he's giving me enough information to try and piece it together myself. I take a moment to mull over everything he's said and try to piece it all together. The moment I understand his meaning, I gasp and stare at him with wide eyes. Crue smiles encouragingly telling me without words to say it aloud.

"Saint can't sign over ownership of Morgan Tech to Devon because he doesn't own it… you do."

"Morgan Tech isn't just owned by me." I frown and cock my head to the side. "We knew Devon would come after Saint, we didn't know how or when, we just knew it would be before his birthday so we needed a fail-safe." His gaze bores into mine with an intensity I've never seen. "Saint knew if Devon hurt him or tried to harm him in any way, I would sign the company over without thought." My eyes widen.

"Oh my God." The smile he wears falters slightly.

"You have to understand, we didn't have a choice and had planned to tell you… eventually."

"I own half of Saint's company," I breathe out.

"Yes. It was the only way to ensure Devon could never get us to sign it over."

"He took my fucking daughter, Crue! How could he not know?" His gaze hardens.

"He thinks he can use her to manipulate Saint into signing everything over to him. Even if Saint wanted to, he can't. You and I own Morgan Tech IT. Devon will never be able to touch what is rightfully Saint's. I think Saint is going to announce this at court, which is why he sent us a warning."

"I'm not following."

"Devon is going to try to come after us, we need to make sure that he doesn't leave that courtroom. We need to meet with the others and come up with a plan to have him charged. I need you to help me find the proof that he was the one who leaked the video of Leah and the pictures of Alexa."

A whoosh of air escapes me. "I can do that." He smiles but I'm about to wipe that off his face. "We need someone to back up that he did do it though, you won't like this but we need Gary to back up what we are saying."

"Oh fuck no. Darius will kill us."

"We don't have a choice. You need to make Darius understand that his brother is the only one who can help us get rid of Saint's father for good."

CHAPTER FIFTEEN

We didn't get in till late last night, and decided that it would be best if we all got a good night's rest before coming up with a plan. I still haven't told Darius about Katie's plan to bring Gary in to help lock Devon's ass up. Katie spent the morning checking out the house, she nearly fainted when I told her I bought the house for the three of us. She shouted and screamed for a good ten minutes before finally calming down enough to register the fact that she has a home here, with us. I know shit is all up in the air with where the three of us stand with each other, and right now I don't have the emotional or mental capacity to deal with that. All I know is, I love them both and want—no, need them with me.

"Leah just text, they're all on their way over." I place my mug in the sink and turn to face her. She stands there nervously wringing her hands in front of herself. Sighing, I make my way over to her and wrap my arms around her, holding her close.

"We have a couple days to get everything set up before we have to go to court. We can do this, Katie baby." She pulls back and cranes her neck back so she can meet my gaze.

"Promise me, that no matter what happens, we don't leave

without Saint and our baby." Gripping her face between my hands I bend until we are eye-to-eye.

"You have my fucking word that Saint and our daughter will be coming home with us on Friday, even if I have to murder every cunt in that courtroom." Relief shines in her eyes before she meshes her mouth to mine. I grip the back of her neck and try to deepen the kiss but the fucking front door opens.

"Oh, should we come back?" Katie pushes away from me and faces our friends with a shy smile and shakes her head. Leah shoots her a wink as she makes her way toward us and fails miserably at whispering, "I want every detail."

"I can hear you," I deadpan.

"So can I!" Darius grits out from a few feet behind her. I motion for everyone to take a seat in the living room. Beck pulls Val onto his lap while Darius and Leah opt to sit on the floor and play with Dawson. Nathan keeps his head down as he follows the others into the living room and opts to lean against the back wall instead of sitting. Alexa walks through the front door looking thoroughly disheveled, her hair a mess and her face is flushed. I'm about to ask if she's okay until I see Corv saunter in behind her. He shoots me a wink.

"You dirty fucker," I tease. He laughs as he makes his way over to give me a hug and then joins Lexi on the couch opposite Beck and Val. I lead Katie over to the other single seat and pull her onto my lap. I look around the room at our friends and smile, but it's forced. It feels wrong him not being here with us. My gaze strays to Dawson and a pang of longing hits me in the chest as my mind begins to wander to my own daughter. What does she look like now? Does she smile often? Would she cry if I held her?

"She'll be home soon," Katie's quietly spoken words have me pulling my gaze from my nephew to stare at her. It's in this moment I realize how much Saint and I fucked up the night we found out she was pregnant.

"I'm so fucking sorry for how we acted and what we said to you that night. We should have been there for you. I'll spend the rest of my life showing you how fucking sorry I am for how we treated you. Adalyn is a gift and I'll never take that for granted again. Forgive me please, Katie baby." Her eyes grow misty with unshed tears as she looks at me, her bottom lip wobbling as she nods her head.

"I love you." Hearing those words out of her mouth has a renewed sense of determination flowing through me to bring our baby and our man home.

"I love you too, always and forever, baby."

"Oh my God." Katie and I both snap our gaze to the others to find Leah and Val both staring at us with open mouths. "That was the cutest fucking thing I have ever heard." Darius groans and rolls his eyes at Leah.

"Jesus Christ, do you want me to get on my hands and fucking knees every day just to please you? Is that what it's gonna take for you to look at me the way you look at Beck and them?" Leah narrows her eyes.

"I don't look at you the way I look at anyone else, because when I look at you, I see my heart. I look at them like this because it's cute to see how happy our friends are. Not everyone is a grumpy prick like you." Her words seem to ease the worry inside my friend. Darius smirks cockily and winks at his girl.

"I know, I just wanted to hear you say that shit in front of your brother." Leah giggles while Corvin flips Darius off.

"Okay, let's focus here and come up with a plan to get Saint and our niece home." Katie sucks in a sharp breath at Beck's acknowledgment of our daughter.

"I think it's time you tell everyone the whole story, babe. They need to know everything," Nathan says from across the room, the sound of his voice grating on my nerves. Katie takes a shuddering breath as she stares at her friend. They look at each other, not saying a word, but it's like they are having a private conversation through their eyes. "I'm right here," he says softly, those three words seem to be what eases her enough to tell her story. I've heard parts but never the whole thing from her point of view.

"Okay." She shoots me a look over her shoulder. I smile encouragingly and nod my head for her to speak her truth. "Okay, after I left here to go home and heal and recover from losing my baby, I started getting sick again, then went to see my doctor only to find out I didn't lose the baby. I had a condition that meant I would bleed throughout my pregnancy. I told Nate, he was only supposed to stay a couple of weeks until I got on my feet, but when he heard the news he chose to stay and help me." That I didn't know. "My family kicked me out, I had no money, no job and I knew the guys didn't want the baby so I thought the only option I had was adoption. I didn't think I would be a good mom and I wanted my baby to have a loving family. I chose to put her up for adoption."

Guilt gnaws at me. I know she thought she wouldn't be a good mom because of the shit Saint and I said to her that night. We had no right to ever project our own shit onto her, we're in this mess because of him and I, not her.

"How did Devon manage to adopt your baby?" Corv asks.

"I chose closed adoption. I thought that way it would be easier so no one would be able to find her and she would be able to live her life happy, loved and with a family that adored her. It wasn't until the day came, I saw Jackson when I had to give her up to go to her new family that I knew something wasn't right. There was nothing I could do, I had just signed over my rights—"

"Yeah, and he signed over ours," I grit out as I pin Nathan with a hateful look. The fucker doesn't back down, he pushes off the wall and moves to stand behind where Corv and Lexi sit on the couch.

"Yes. I did that because I thought I was doing what was

right not only Katie but for Adalyn as well. Maybe if you and Saint had pulled your heads out of your asses and didn't accuse her of trying to trap you, or making her believe that she would be a shit mom because she didn't know which of you fuckers was her baby daddy, things would have been different." I tense and grit my teeth. What he says is true, we did say some fucked up shit.

"Nate—"

He cuts Katie off. "No, they need to hear it. You can hate me all you want but you weren't fucking there," he roars. "I picked up the fucking pieces of her heart when you both abandoned her on the floor of her dorm, then when her parents disowned her, I picked her up. I was there for the pregnancy and all the scares she had when she thought she lost Addy each time she bled. I held her hand through the birth. I was the fucking one who tried to convince her she was worthy of that little girl and promised to care for her and Addy as if they were my own. You and Saint can both choke on my dick and shove your judgment up your asses, because I did what any good fucking friend would do."

I sit here with my mouth open staring at Nathan, shocked and speechless for a moment. "You tried to keep… Adalyn?" I breathe out.

"Yes, asshole. Regardless of what you both thought, I knew my girl would be an amazing mother to that little girl. We may be poor and struggle weekly to make ends meet but we would have made it work. I would have made sure that Katie and Addy had everything they needed, even if it meant I had to drop out of school and work full-time to provide for them both." I lift Katie off my lap and stand, she darts in front of me pushing against my chest.

"Don't you dare touch him!" she shouts as Darius, Beck and Corv all leap to their feet. I grab Katie's wrists and meet her gaze so she can see the truth in my eyes.

"I'm not, I swear." I release her and move toward Nathan.

The guys all follow me but I ignore them. Nathan straightens the moment I stop an inch away from him. Before he can say a word, I draw the fucker in for a hug and say low enough for only him to hear.

"Thank you for being there for them both when we couldn't. We owe you more than we can repay. You have my word that I will do whatever it takes to get Adalyn back and make Katie happy."

"Just be good for them both and then your debt to me is repaid," he says. We pull apart but maintain eye contact. Nathan owed none of us anything and yet, time and again he has proven to be there for each of these girls and shows up to pick up the pieces whenever we fuck up. He really is a good guy.

"You got it." He nods, but I can see it in the depths of his green eyes he thinks I'm talking out my ass. That's fine, I'll prove him wrong over time.

"You should also know, Jackson has been doing back door shady shit that Katie has info on. If you plan to take down Devon, then you're gonna need the dirt Katie has on that prick."

I snort. "Don't think much of my cousin either, huh?" I tease.

Nathan rolls his eyes. "He's a slimy piece of shit that needs to be taken down a peg or ten."

My gaze softens. "He treated you badly because of your sexual preference, didn't he?"

Nate's gaze hardens. "Yes. I don't expect everyone to be okay with who I am, but I also won't tolerate someone using my preference of bed partners to paint me as a bad parent and say that Adalyn would be better without my influence in her life."

My jaw unhinges. "He said that?" I ask.

"No, he wrote it in the report he drafted for the adoption.

We didn't know until after I hacked his phone and got the passcodes," Katie says.

"That motherfucker is going down for fucking with one of ours," Darius grits out. Fuck yes, he is. Nathan is one of us and we protect our own.

CHAPTER SIXTEEN

Katie

"Fuck no!" Darius shouts as he continues to pace the living room. Ever since I told him that we needed Gary to come forward and admit that he was able to upload the video and distribute it across the net through Saint's dad's company, he has been going off. "That cunt doesn't come near us. None of us have heard from him for months and it needs to stay that way." Leah stands and moves to step in front of him to stop his pacing, but he shakes his head and steps out of her reach.

"Halfback—"

"No, Goldie. That cunt needs to be in a box under the fucking dirt. He doesn't come near you, ever!" The anguish in tone has me feeling like an asshole for suggesting this but without hard proof, it's all hearsay in the eyes of the law. Leah softens and moves toward him again, this time he doesn't back away from her when she wraps her arms around his waist and looks up at him.

"He won't be near me. You and my brother will be by my side the entire time. He can't hurt me anymore, halfback." Darius sighs and leans down resting his forehead against hers. Normally, Corvin would make a snarky remark at how close they are but even he knows Darius needs this. Leah is the only one who will be able to convince him to change his mind and help us find his twin.

"I hate this," he says quietly.

"I know. I don't relish the idea of seeing him either, but Saint needs us to do this. We'll never have to see him again after this. Our friend needs us. Please Darius, we can't let our hang-up with that piece of shit stand in the way of bringing them home."

A whoosh of air escapes him as he closes his eyes and breathes Leah in, it's amazing to see how she is able to calm the bad boy down. "Fine. But you stay by my side the entire time. If he says one fucking word to you or even looks your way, he's dead."

"Deal," she rushes to say before planting a kiss on his lips.

"Okay, so what's next?" Beck asks.

"We prove Devon is a liar and get his ass arrested, then we overturn the adoption," Crue says. Nate tenses from his spot beside me.

"We need to tread carefully with that," I cut in, everyone turns toward Nathan and me.

"Why?" Alexa asks.

"Because Nathan forged the documents and said he was Adalyn's father. I lied on legal documents as well if it comes down to it." I take a deep breath and push on. "But, Nate and I are willing to be charged for fraud if it means bringing Addy and Saint home." Crue's face morphs into one of panic.

"No, that isn't happening. We'll figure this shit out. We just need to prove Devon is guilty, come out as the owners of Morgan Tech IT so he can't go after Saint, then Adalyn will be useless to him." I try to smile to reassure Crue. Truth is, we need a lawyer and unfortunately Troy has gone radio silent.

"I know a lawyer." I dart my gaze to Lexi and frown, she shrugs her shoulders. "You said that out loud."

"Oh," is all I manage to say.

"How do you know a lawyer?" Corv asks, clearly surprised.

"Reaper, my uncle is a lawyer. I can give him a call if you want?" I nod eagerly.

"Since when do you have an uncle, jail bait?" Corvin sounds pissed he is only learning this information now.

Lex rolls her eyes as she turns to her man. "Reaper, I didn't think you would want to know about my uncle since my cousin Lacey is in a relationship with her three stepbrothers." Corvin's face morphs into one of outrage.

"You're cutting your cousin out and never speaking to her again." We all laugh at Corvin's expense.

"Whatever you say, babe," Lex says as she dials her uncle and puts the call on speaker as we all crowd around her.

He answers on the fourth ring. "Alexa, how are you, my sweet girl?" I can tell from the bright smile on her face that she is very fond of her uncle.

"Hi, Uncle John. I'm good, thanks. I'm sorry to call you out of the blue like this—"

"Don't you dare be sorry, you know you can call me anytime you like."

"Thanks, Uncle John."

"Now, I don't want to be presumptuous but I'm assuming this isn't a catch-up call?" Lexi cringes.

"Uh, yeah, sorry. I kind of need some help."

"What do you need?" The way he doesn't hesitate to help her tells me he really does care about his niece, pity her parents didn't feel the same way. Alexa tells him everything and by the time she has finished explaining the situation, she is breathless. "Okay, well, first thing first. The lawyer friend you have, is he representing you guys or your other friend?"

Lexi looks to us and honestly, I have no idea who Troy is working with. "I think it's safe to say Saint will be using Troy," Crue says.

"Okay, I'll book a flight and be there for the court date. We are going to say that you were coerced into signing over the rights to the child. Jackson manipulated you and Nathan into signing over your rights and promised there would be no blowback on either of you." He then continues to explain his tactics and how he plans to proceed with the case. John really knows what he is doing which helps calm my nerves.

"Thank you so much, Uncle John. Corvin and I will pick you up from the airport," Lexi says.

"See you then, my dear," he says before ending the call. I launch myself at Lexi and hug her tight.

"Thank you. I don't know what we would have done without you." She laughs and hugs me back before pulling away and pinning me with a look.

"That was the easy part. You need to find this Gary guy now," she says.

"Don't worry, I know where he is," Darius says somberly from the other side of the room. Well, that shocks the shit out of all of us.

"You've been keeping tabs on him?" Beckett accuses.

Darius pins Beck with a scathing look. "I told you I would protect Leah and never let him hurt her again. In order to do that, I had to know where he was at all times."

"We need to get to Gary and make sure he'll even testify," Crue says.

"He'll testify, don't worry," Darius says as he heads for the door. Before he can leave, Corvin grips his arm and yanks him around to face him.

"Where the fuck are you going?" Corv snaps.

"To go get the cunt that came from the same nut sack as I did." I cover my laughter by coughing.

"Not by yourself, we're coming with you," Beck says. Crue comes and gives me a kiss, promising to call me when they have Gary. We stand here and watch the four of them leave, it's so strange not seeing Saint amongst them. It's always been the five of them since the first time I saw them all in the quad. Little did I know back then that I would be welcomed into the inner circle of the kings of CHU's homes and hearts. They were untouchable, girls would do anything to get their attention, and guys longed to be in their presence. I thought they were shallow, selfish pricks but after getting to know them, I saw how wrong I was. These guys have the biggest hearts and love harder than anyone I know.

It's been over an hour since the guys left and the tension in the house is at a peak. The five of us sit in the living room watching some cartoon with Dawson. If you asked me what the show was about, I wouldn't be able to tell you, I've been too lost in my own thoughts to even pay attention. My phone chimes with an incoming text. All heads turn to me as I pull it out and unlock it. The message is from an unknown number. My breath hitches when I open the messages thread.

UNKNOWN

I'm bringing her home.

Below the text is a picture of a smiling baby girl, blue eyes and blonde hair with a tiny button nose. Tears immediately cascade down my cheeks at the sight of my daughter. I know without a doubt that the message is from Saint, he's telling me that they're okay and he's doing everything he can to get back to us and bring our girl home where she belongs.

"Katie, what happened?" The worry in Val's voice has me snapping out of it and swiping my tears away as I turn to face my friends. I turn my phone to them so they can see, the four of them rush toward me and fight to get a better look.

"Is that her?"

"Oh my God, she's beautiful."

"She looks like you."

"Addy girl," they all say in unison, and the love I hear in

each of their voices fills me with hope. One day, when she is older, I'll have to explain all this to her and I just hope that Adalyn will be able to forgive me for making the biggest mistake of my life.

"That's our little girl," I say proudly. The girl's faces melt, Nate smiles proudly at me.

"You got this, Momma." He may not know it, but his words have a renewed strength flowing through me. I am her momma and it's my job to make sure she is safe.

An idea hits me then. "How would you all feel about helping me turn one of the spare rooms into a nursery for her?" That's all it takes for Val, Leah and Nate to start throwing ideas around, Lexi looks horrified at the thought of going baby shopping. Within ten minutes the five of us and Dawson are heading out, we pile into Val's Range Rover and head for the mall. Excitement fills me, I never got the chance to do this when I was pregnant so to be able to do it now with my best friends with me is a feeling I can't describe. We've all been so fixated on the court case that none of us thought to worry about a crib, clothes, Pampers or anything.

Pulling up to the mall, Val parks the car and we all amble out ready to shop. It's then that I remember, I can't afford to be doing this. I freeze in the middle of the parking lot, it takes a minute for the others to realize I'm not following before they turn back.

"What's wrong?" Lexi asks. I'm too ashamed to meet her gaze so I just shake my head.

"Bitch, use your damn words!" Nate snaps sassily. I dart my gaze to his and glare.

"This was a stupid idea."

"What, why?" Leah asks with concern thick in her tone.

"I can't afford to do this, I'm sorry, can we just go?" I say as I turn, ready to head back to the car but Val's words stop me.

"Oh, hell no. You listen to me, Katie. I've been where you

are. We are going to go shopping and spoil the shit out of our niece so you can either sit in the car and sulk or you can come help us pick things out for Addy. Think of it as our belated baby shower gifts. Plus, I promised Beck I would get you guys everything you needed for the baby." To say I am fucking grateful for these amazing women is an understatement, I'm so blessed to have each of these girls in my life. Nate bumps his shoulder into mine and winks.

"Who are we to deny them the chance to spoil our girl and you never know, they may take pity on us poor folk and buy us that Gucci bag we love." I gape up at him.

"*You* want that Gucci bag, not me," I admonish. He just rolls his eyes and waves me off.

"Bitch, please, I helped you birth that watermelon. Aunty Nate deserves an expensive gift for having to see your vagina be destroyed."

Fucking hell, trust Nathan to have us all laughing to the point of tears. "I'll buy you the bag, babe," Leah says through her laughter. Fuck, I really needed this time with my girls. I missed them so much.

CHAPTER SEVENTEEN

Pulling up around the back of the court house, my nerves begin to get the better of me. It feels fucking amazing to finally be home. We got in late last night as Devon refused to fly in any earlier, claiming that being back in the US wasn't good for him. It took more self-control than I thought I had to not laugh at the prick. He flew first class and forced me to fly coach, or he wouldn't allow me to keep Adalyn with me. Needless to say, I wore a baseball cap and hood the entire plane ride so no one recognized me and snapped a pic while I'm covered head to toe in bruises. David—Devon's head of security—puts the car in park before he and the other three guards get out, leaving Devon, me and Addy alone in the car. He turns sideways and peers over the back of his seat, watching as I pull Addy out of her car seat and carefully place her in the baby carrier that is attached to my front without waking her.

"Do as I said and you walk out with your bastard." I bite down on my tongue to keep from ripping him a new one and nod. He eyes me for a moment longer and I can tell he doesn't trust me to keep my word and say what he wants me to. "Don't fuck this up or I'll make sure your other leg is broken." My nostrils flare in anger. Yes, my right leg is in a moon boot but it's only a fracture thanks to that cunt David taking a baseball to my ankle the night they beat my ass nearly a week ago.

"Wouldn't dream of it," I force past clenched teeth. Devon thinks I'm about to stand in court and say that Katie is lying so he can retain custody of Addy. Truth is, none of them have any idea what I'm about to do in there.

"Let's get this over with," he snarls, then raps his knuckles against the window. The door is opened for him. It takes effort on my part to climb from the back in a moon boot with a baby strapped to my front. None of them offer a hand as I climb out, then reach back in for the nappy bag that I sling over my shoulder. Addy hasn't been settling for a couple days since we ran out of Katie's breast milk. She doesn't like the formula so I'm hoping to get this shit over with so my baby can finally eat from her mother.

Six guards surround us as we make our way to the front. My steps falter when I see them standing out the front of the court house. The closer we get the harder it gets to keep my mask in place. If I slip up now, he'll take Addy and run. I need to do this. He bought my daughter and I have the proof that him and Jackson never went through the right channels for the adoption. Katie's eyes fill with tears when our eyes meet. She looks to the tiny bundle strapped to my chest and tries to come to me, but Crue wraps an arm around her waist, holding her back. Beck, Darius and Corvin all look to me with blank looks on their faces. They know me and know I wouldn't be here with this cunt if I didn't have to be.

"Saint, please," Katie begs as we pass by. I keep my gaze ahead and ignore her. The moment I hear her begin to sob and shout for me to give her Addy I nearly crumble, until Devon places a hand on my shoulder and laughs.

"Don't worry, boy, you'll never have to deal with that sissy and that whore again. You get to keep the bastard and do whatever the fuck you want after we get this shit over with." If I didn't have my baby strapped to my chest, I would have punched this asshole in the mouth for speaking about them like that. "Make sure you let the courts know that you recant your statement you made to the news. Tell them I adopted her legally and that everything is above board."

"Of course, pops," I say with way too much fake enthusiasm as we enter the courtroom. Devon leads the way toward the front. I spy Troy next to Devon's lawyer and keep my face blank as Devon introduces us.

"Saint, meet Colin Vaughn and Troy Hughes." I reach out and shake each of their hands.

"You okay, kid?" Troy asks.

"He's fine, just being a punk and got into some trouble, right son?" Devon answers for me. I force a smile.

"Yeah, my mouth seems to get me in shit, as Pop said." Troy nods and acts like the sight of my bruised face doesn't bother him but I can see in his eyes, he's fucking furious and knows who is responsible for it. How Devon has no fucking idea that Troy has been on retainer for us for years, I have no fucking idea. I mean, the guy was there when we announced we were the owners of BCD'S.

I take a seat on the pew as Devon speaks in hushed tones with his lawyers. I spy out of the corner of my eye Beck, Corv, Darius, Crue, Katie, Lexi, Nathan, and Leah sliding into the row opposite me. I fight the frown from breaking free at the sight of a girl who looks similar to Alexa slip in beside Leah with two guys, they're fucking twins! A middle-aged man with salt and pepper hair pushes through the little gates and heads for the desk opposite Troy's, then turns and speaks to my friends but I can't hear a word. I quickly turn away from them, hating that I'm stuck on this side. I look down at my little girl and wonder how a father couldn't love their own flesh and blood.

Devon Morgan is a heartless bastard. How can he stand

here with his head held high knowing he bought his own granddaughter to use as a pawn just so he could manipulate his own son into signing over everything he was meant to inherit? My mother left the stipulation in her will that I had to be running the company by my twenty-first birthday in order for Devon to get a cut. She hated him as much as I do from what he's told me and that was her way of making sure I would always be okay financially.

I could never do that to Adalyn.

"All rise." Silence descends over the room as we all stand for the judge and wait for her to be seated before we claim our seats again.

"Councilors, you're on the docket for the case of Morgan Vs Hastings," the judge says.

"Yes, your honor, my client is prepared to not press any charges against Mr. Hastings and the birth mother of his daughter if they drop all the accusations against him and agree to pay the sum of five hundred thousand dollars for slandering him online," Devon's lawyer says.

"Your honor, my clients have informed me that Mr. Morgan did not proceed through the correct adoption channels and be vetted for the adoption."

"What are you saying, Mr. Sutton?" The judge asks as she leans forward in her seat.

"Mr. Morgan paid a member of the agency, Mr. Jackson Rathborne to obtain the care of the child—"

"Where's your proof?" Devon's lawyer demands. I know without him saying it, he has none because Katie hacked Jackson's computer illegally.

"We were informed from a reliable source," their lawyer states.

"Is your source here?" the lawyer taunts. Sutton's eyes narrow.

"No," he grits out through clenched teeth.

"Without proof, Mr. Sutton, your accusations are nothing

but hearsay," the judge announces. I spy Katie out of the corner of my eye trying to stand, my eyes widen the moment I see Crue clamp a hand over her mouth to keep her quiet. "Without any proof, there is no case here. This is a closed adoption that the mother and the father both signed away their rights. The child in question shouldn't even be in the courtroom." I shoot the bitch a glare. "I'm inclined to rule in favor of Mr. Morgan receiving compensation for his time and the stress this must have caused him." The judge bangs her gavel and calls for the next case. Devon shakes his lawyer's hands, I look to my friends, they all look shocked and fucking furious.

"Let's go, boy," Devon says as he tries to pass by me but I stop him with a hand to his chest.

"No can-do, Pops, we're the next case."

"Gentlemen, would you care to explain why you are my next case?" the judge asks. Devon's gaze bores into mine, I smile wide as I whisper low enough for only him to hear.

"I won, motherfucker. Enjoy rotting in a cell, you piece of shit."

"Yes, your honor," Troy says as he moves across to the other side of the room and stands next to Mr. Sutton. "We are here to appeal to the court to terminate the rights of Mr. Devon Morgan as the Guardian of Adalyn Faith Hastings-Morgan."

"You can't do that!" Devon shouts.

"Sit down, Mr. Morgan, another outburst like that and I will have you remanded into custody." Devon grits his teeth and nods as he lowers into his seat. "I want to know why you are wasting my time Mr. Hughes?"

Troy nods and starts grabbing papers from his briefcase. He motions for one of the guys standing at the side of the courtroom to come and grab them. The guy hands the papers to the judge as Troy begins to explain. "As you can see there in front of you, the child in question was adopted illegally.

Mr. Morgan and Mr. Rathborne are both linked to numerous illegal adoptions." Devon stiffens beside me. I got you this time motherfucker.

"This is all well and good counselor but how was this obtained?" the judge asks.

"I would like to call a witness to the stand, your honor, who will be able to explain."

"I'm not in the habit of going against court protocol but given the alarming information in these documents, I'll allow it this time." Troy nods.

"I'd like to call Saint Morgan to the stand." My friends all gasp as I climb to my feet. Devon grips my hand, drawing my gaze back to him.

"I'll end that bastard and you, boy," he hisses low enough for only me to hear.

I yank my hand free. "You will be rotting a cell by the end of the day, you bastard," I seethe as I turn and make my way to the stand.

"Uh, Mr. Morgan, I cannot allow a child to take the stand with you." I nod my head. Devon stands thinking I'll hand Addy to him, stupid fuck. I undo the carrier and step toward Crue and Katie,. They both stare up at me with wide eyes as I gently hand Addy to Crue.

"Trust me, I swear I have a plan," I whisper as Crue cradles Addy against his chest, the look on his face as he stares down at our daughter is a look I'll never forget. I can't look at Katie or I'll crumble. I make my way to the stand and swear my oath on the bible before I take a seat and wait for Troy to question me. I see Devon and his lawyer speaking in hushed tones, trying to come up with a plan to get his ass out of this mess. He can't, not this time.

"Mr. Morgan, can you please state your name, relationship to the defendant, and your relationship to the child for the record of the courts."

I do as Troy says. "My name is Saint Morgan. Devon

Morgan is my father and my relationship with Adalyn Hastings-Morgan is…" My gaze strays to Crue and Katie, they both stare at me with worry in each of their gazes. What I'm about to say next is going to change things, but it will never change how I feel toward her. "Glorified uncle." Crue's eyes are the size of dinner plates and tears fill Katie's. I turn to my father and smile, trump card, motherfucker.

Adalyn isn't my daughter biologically.

"Can you explain how you were able to obtain the information that was just presented to the court?"

"Yes. While I was staying with my father, who admitted to me himself that Adalyn was adopted illegally, I was granted access to his computer which is when I stumbled upon all the information that was just presented. I also learned that before my company, BCD'S which I co-own with my best friends, acquired my father's company, he was also distributing illegal videos of underage children and selling them through his app, *EyeSpy*."

Gasps sound out around the court. If looks could kill, the way Devon is looking at me would see me burnt at the stake. "You have evidence of this confession?" Devon's lawyer cuts in and asks.

"Well, yes, we do actually," Troy says. "With your permission, your honor, I'd like to submit this thumb drive into evidence for the court to review."

"Granted," she says. Troy hands the thumb drive to one of the guys who hooks it up to the TV screen at the side of the room. The video begins to play and rather than relive that moment, I look to Crue and Katie and mouth *don't watch*.

CHAPTER EIGHTEEN

Don't watch, he mouths. I shake my head as I need to see everything he went through in order for us to get to this point. Bruises still mar his handsome face, and the moon boot he wears scares the shit out of me. What the fuck happened to him? The video begins to play and the sound of Devon's angry tone fills the room.

"Sign the papers boy," he growls.

"Not until you sign her over to me."

I gasp as we watch six large men enter the room and fan out around Saint. He looks at each of them and when a look of acceptance crosses his face, my heart breaks, he knows what's about to happen to him. He leans down and places a kiss on Addy's little head before nodding for… it's the lady from the hotel. She comes and takes Addy from Saint. The moment they disappear from the room, Saint cracks his neck side to side and looks to his father.

"Let's get this beating over with, shall we?"

"It doesn't have to be this way, you're a star now, boy. You really want pictures of you snapped and posted online covered in bruises?"

"We gonna keep playing with our dicks or get this shit over because I'm not signing anything, motherfucker."

"Teach him a lesson," Devon snarls.

I watch in horror as the six men all rush Saint. He does his best to fight back but there are too many of them. He covers his head with his arms as he drops to the ground, grunting in pain. Beck, Corvin, Darius, Crue, Nathan and even Alexa's cousins' boyfriends, Tanner and Talon, are all grunting and growling at the injustice that Saint is being subjected to. The moment Devon hands one of the guys a baseball bat, I die inside.

"Oh, my God," I cry as I watch the guy use the bat on Saint's leg. The scream of pain that comes from him fucking kills me.

"I'm coming for you, motherfucker," Darius shouts at Devon.

"You son of a fucking bitch!" Crue roars from beside me, the judge pins them with a warning look but even she looks disgusted by the video. The men step away from Saint to reveal my bloody, beaten and bruised, strong man lying there on the ground broken. Sobs can be heard from the girls but I'm too transfixed on the screen to look at them. Devon kneels down beside Saint, tears trek down my cheeks when I see he's still conscious. A part of me hoped they had knocked him out so he wouldn't have felt the full force of their kicks and punches.

"Sign the company and your inheritance over to me and I'll give you that bastard. The courts will rule in favor since you're my son and it's my bastard granddaughter." Anger thrums through me at how he speaks about my child. Crue grinds his teeth so fucking hard to try to control himself from lashing out at Devon.

Even broken and beaten, Saint smiles a bloody smile up at his father. *"You dumb fuck, you will never get a single cent. You fucked up the moment you went to Jackson and adopted my daughter illegally, I never signed my rights over. Katie's friend lied and forged those documents."* Horror fills me as I look to Nathan who has turned pale, we're going to jail. *"Do whatever you want to me, I don't care. All I want is my daughter."*

Hearing those words come from his lips has hope blossoming inside my chest, maybe him knowing the truth about Addy not being his won't change things.

"Give me everything I want and then I'll give it to you."

"Sign her over to me and relinquish your rights, then I'll give you everything."

A dark laugh escapes Devon. *"Nice try. Tell the court you knew about the adoption and agreed to it and then sign over the ownership of the company and everything else to me, I'll give you what you want. Fuck me over and I'll make sure that mutt pays the price."*

The video ends and I slowly turn back to Saint. Sadness shines in his eyes but it isn't for himself, he's sad we had to see what he went through to get here.

"Your honor, I move to petition the court to have Mr. Devon Morgan arrested and charged with the assault, fraud, and illegal distribution of child pornography—"

"You have no proof of that distribution," Devon's lawyer argues.

"Actually," John begins cutting in before Troy can. "We have a witness that can attest to these claims."

"Very well, Mr. Sutton," The judge says. "Mr. Morgan, you may step down," She says to Saint. He limps back toward us and instead of returning to his original seat he slips into the row behind us and rests a hand atop each of Crue's and my shoulders. "Call your witness, counselor."

"We call Gary Hayes to the stand." Saint's grip on my shoulder tightens, clearly he's surprised we were able to build our own case.

"You're not the only one with tricks up your sleeve," Crue whispers over his shoulder. Gary walks into the courtroom looking like a shell of the guy I saw at the game the night he played that video. He's skinny and looks rugged. We wait with bated breath as Gary is sworn in and takes his seat, his gaze never once strays our way. I look over to Leah to find Darius and Beck have both pushed in closer to her. Darius holds her hand while Beck has his arm wrapped around her shoulders.

"Mr. Hayes, please state your name for the court," John asks.

"Uh, Gary Hayes."

"What is your relationship to the defendant?" John continues.

"Um, Devon was friends with my dad."

"Is that the only way you know Mr. Morgan?" Troy pushes.

Gary sucks in a breath and shakes his head, his gaze briefly strays to Darius for a second before focusing back on Troy. "No, his son's football team and mine had a rivalry. I've known Saint since high school."

"It's my understanding that this *rivalry* became dangerous and involved a video of an underage girl, is that correct?"

It takes Gary a second to answer John's question. "Yes. I… I… I slept with the rival QB's little sister." Corvin growls.

"This girl wasn't just the QB's little sister though, was she?" Troy hedges.

Gary sighs, "No. Leah Williams is my… She's my…" He scrubs a hand down his face before continuing. "She's my brother's girlfriend, but at the time I had no idea Darius was my brother."

"But your father and Mr. Morgan knew exactly who Darius was to you, didn't they?" Gary grits his teeth and nods. "I need you to say the words, Mr. Hayes," Troy urges.

"Yes. Devon and my dad knew about Darius. I didn't find out until… after that Darius is my twin."

"Is it true that Mr. Morgan reached out to you and offered

you the use of his app to distribute the video of you and Miss Williams in the *act,* so that it would have a further reach?" John asks.

"Yes. When Devon overheard me talking to a couple of my teammates while he was at my house, he said I could use *EyeSpy* so the video would go further and reach more people than just posting it on social media." Gary is excused from the stand, shooting Darius one last look before he exits the courtroom.

"Given the circumstance and the severity of this case, I'm ruling that Mr. Morgan and the men in that video be charged and reprimanded until a court date can be set for sentencing." Devon and his men begin to shout and scream as guards come in and start ushering them out. Relief surges through me, this is finally over. "In regards to the forged documentation of the paternity of the child, I'm taking the mother and the supposed father noted on the birth certificate into custody." My friends begin to shout as I sit here in shock, I'm going to jail. Nate is going to do time because of me. The judge starts banging her gavel demanding order. Addy wakes and begins to cry, without thinking I snatch her off Crue and hold her against my chest as I try to soothe my baby.

"Your honor, we would also like to appeal to the court in regards to the adoption," John rushes to say after my friends sit down and shut their mouths.

"Make this quick, Mr. Sutton," she grits out.

"Katie and Nathan were both coerced into signing the adoption papers. Jackson was well aware that Nathan wasn't the father of the child and I have email receipts between him and Mr. Morgan to prove that." Shock ripples through me as I place kisses on the top of my girl's head. "With a warrant, we were able to seize Mr. Rathborne's computer at his office and his private laptop and garner access to his emails. Mr. Morgan isn't the only… client he has dealt with."

"Where is Mr. Rathborne at this time?" the judge asks.

"He's currently in jail in Tennessee awaiting charges," Troy answers. Crue turns to peer over his shoulder at Saint.

"You didn't think I would let that bitch go free, did you?" Saint cockily asks.

"I understand what you are saying here, Mr. Hughes, but until this can be resolved in front of a jury both of them need to be held and the child needs to be taken to—" Before she finishes Crue is on his feet.

"I'm her father. I had nothing to do with adoption, she stays with me."

The judge narrows her eyes at Crue. "Mr. Hastings, I cannot allow that—"

"Your honor, with all due respect. I don't care what you think you can allow. Adalyn is my daughter. I've been fighting for months to get her back because of that sick bastard thinking he could use her to manipulate my best friend into signing over his company."

I place a kiss on my little girl's nose as she smiles up at me, a lump forms in my throat. "I love you, Addy," I whisper as I stand and hand her to Saint, he eyes me skeptically but takes her from me.

"If Adalyn gets to leave with her father, I'll stay and be remanded." My guys and our friends all begin to shout and argue but I push on. "Nathan only signed the papers because I tricked him." Nate tries to argue but I talk louder so she hears me over him. "He didn't know what he was signing, I lied to him. I forged the documentation for the adoption, not Nate. Saint, and Crue had nothing to do with any of this."

Everything happens in a blur, I can't hear anything over the blood pounding in my ears after the judge banged her gavel and ordered the guards to arrest me. Crue tries to grab me but the guys hold him back as the guards pull my arms behind my back and cuff me. Saint tries to get to me but the girls scream at him to stop because of the baby. I'm so thankful that he chooses to stop and not risk injuring Addy to get to me. The sight of her with them fills me with warmth. I fucked up and now I need to do the time for the crime I committed.

"I swear to God, I'll get you out," Nathan shouts as the guards lead me away.

"Katie." I peer over my shoulder at the sound of Saint's voice. "We're coming for you." The conviction in his tone is awe-inspiring. I know without a doubt that they will do whatever they can to get me out. Well, I hope so because let's be real, they got what they wanted. They did say the moment they got Addy back I was no longer welcome.

It's hard not to doubt their love for me when they are the ones who left me the first time.

CHAPTER NINETEEN

Watching her be carted off in handcuffs will forever be seared into my memories for the rest of my life. Fuck, the hopeless look in her eyes as she looked at Saint killed me. I saw it, the doubt. She doesn't know if she can trust us to keep our word and get her out. We'll prove her ass wrong, there is no way I'm going to let the mother of our child rot in a cell because of what we did to her. This whole fucking clusterfuck of events is on me and Saint. The reaction we had to finding out she was pregnant was fucking disgusting and honestly, I'm so ashamed of myself for the things I said and did.

"I've set a bail hearing for first thing on Monday," Troy says, pulling me from my thoughts. I turn away from the crib where Addy is sleeping and look to our lawyer. Saint is leaning against the far wall with his arms crossed over his chest. Darius, Beck and Corv all stand behind Troy in the doorway.

"She can't stay there the whole weekend" I snap.

Troy sighs. "I'm sorry, Crue, but not even money can buy her way out of this one. I'm having Jackson transferred here to stand trial. The only thing we can do is offer to drop some charges against Jackson if he confesses to manipulating Katie and Nathan into signing the forms."

"He wasn't even there," Saint adds. "She said she had no idea he was involved until after they came to collect Addy."

"We know that but the courts don't. From the minimal interaction I've had with Jackson I can see he is a self-serving son of a bitch and I can almost guarantee he would be willing to perjure himself on the stand if it meant serving a lighter sentence." I turn from the others and stare down at Adalyn. Looking at her now, I can't believe I nearly lost her.

"Do whatever you have to do in order to bring Katie home. Whatever it costs, whatever you need it's yours. Just bring our girl home."

Even as the sun begins to set, the five of us guys sit on the ground and watch Addy sleep. We're all eager to feed her, hold her, kiss her little cheeks, or just do anything with her the moment she wakes. Saint told us how she doesn't like the formula. I put in a request with Troy to see if there was a way to get a pump to Katie so we could use her milk. I know being in there without that pump would be agony for her.

"Can you still play?" Corvin's question breaks the silence in the room. Saint stares down at his leg for a moment before focusing back on Corv.

"I hope so. The doctor back in New Zealand said it was a fracture. I guess, I'll just have to wait and see." Saint and I haven't even had a chance to discuss the news of Addy not being his and where this leaves us. I don't even know where we both stand with Katie, all I care about right now is getting her home so our family can be whole again.

"Nearly five years ago, I met some punk kids at a high school I had just enrolled in after running away from a murder I just committed. Little did I know at that time that I would end up here, buying a row of houses side by side just so we could stay close even when we all don't live here full time." We chuckle at Beck, he isn't wrong. I never saw us being here.

"We were just a bunch of punk-ass teenagers with Mommy and Daddy issues who set out to start a business we had no idea how to run, just so we could make enough money to say fuck you to them. Now look at us." Darius is right. This was about making something of ourselves so our parents could eat shit and realize we aren't fuck ups.

"Everything worked out just how we planned. We took down Darius's dad, Devon is behind bars and not getting out anytime soon. We all have enough money to last us five life-times. We each achieved our dreams, got the girls and now we get to live the life we always dreamed of." Corvin's words have me feeling nostalgic. I look around at each of these guys —we went from being friends to best friends and then, over time, they became my brothers. I would lay down my life for each of them without thought, they are my chosen family.

"The only thing missing from this moment is my baby momma," I say and look right at Saint. The moment he grins back at me, the tension slowly bleeds out of me.

"*Our* baby momma, prick." That one word, *our*, is all it takes for me to know that nothing has changed and nothing will change. He doesn't view Addy differently because she isn't his biologically.

"I got to know, did you really get that video and the DNA shit done?" Beck asks Saint.

"Simple, I knew the very first moment I saw Adalyn that she was Crue's, she looks exactly like him. The maid hated how Devon treated Addy and when she saw what he did to me she gave me the passcodes to his security room where I snagged the footage. The day she went to see Crue and Katie, she dropped off the cotton swabs I used to test Addy and me to the lab, the results were sent to Troy." I stare at him in shock.

"Why?" Darius breathes out.

"I knew the moment Devon learned that Addy didn't share my DNA he wouldn't have a chance as claiming her. Crue being her bio dad meant the courts couldn't hold her and put her in the system until we figured out the court case."

"So, I'm gonna ask what we're all thinking, what the fuck are the two of you and Katie?" Saint and I share a look, I answer for both of us.

"We're us, no labels needed. She's ours and we're hers, that's it."

"Does she know that?" At the sound of Katie's voice in the doorway we're all jumping to our feet. Saint and I rush her and crush her against us in an awkward three-way hug. Katie melts into us and fuck, I'll admit I get choked up. This is the first time the three of us have been together in the same house with our daughter. The feeling of having my family together is a feeling like none other.

"Let her breathe, assholes." Laughter bubbles out of me at Beck's smartass comment. We step away from Katie, letting the guys in. They each give her a hug and tell her how glad they are to have her home.

"Thanks, but if you don't mind, I'm gonna go see my daughter now," she says hesitantly as she flicks her gaze to Saint and me. We both nod and try to smile reassuringly. The five of us watch as she gently lifts Addy out of her crib and nuzzles her face. I smile when Addy begins to coo at her mom. The moment Katie sits down in the rocking chair in the corner and starts to lift her shirt to feed, Saint and I snap into action.

"Get the fuck out."

"Close your fucking eyes," we both shout in unison. Corv, Beck and Darius burst out laughing as they back out of the room, shouting their goodbyes and promising to check in later as I shut the door.

"Sorry," her quietly spoken word draws our attention back to her. My eyes widen at the sight of our girl latched onto Katie's breast. Saint sighs beside me.

"She hasn't eaten properly in days." Katie frowns.

"Why?"

"She doesn't like formula. I ran out of the supply you sent a couple days ago." She nods and goes back to staring down at our little one as she eats. Don't get me wrong, I'm not turned on or anything, but the sight of her feeding Adalyn from her breast is a fucking beautiful sight to see. She not only carried and nurtured this amazing little girl but she's also able to give her sustenance from her own body, that's fucking amazing. Silence stretches between us and the tension in the room is so thick you cut it with a butter knife.

Katie unlatches Adalyn when she falls asleep. She rests her little chin on her shoulder as she covers herself up and begins to tap gently on her back. Contentment can be seen in her features as she closes her eyes and rocks back and forth burping the tiny human we created. Saint and I just stand here and watch them. When it becomes apparent Katie has fallen asleep, I lean in close to Saint and whisper,

"Put Addy in her crib, I'll carry Katie to bed." Nodding, he gently lifts Addy off Katie and places her in the crib, while I gently lift Katie into my arms. She immediately nuzzles into my chest as I walk us next door to our room. Saint limps around me and draws the covers back as I lay her on the bed. He takes her shoes off before I tuck her in. I motion with my head for him to follow me out of the room.

Saint grabs each of us a beer before sliding onto the stool next to me at the breakfast counter in the kitchen. "How is she here?" I ask.

"Fucked if I know and honestly, I don't care. I'm just

fucking happy she's here." My phone begins to ring. I pull it out of my pocket and snort when I see it's Troy calling.

I answer the call and place it on speaker. "Forget to tell us a surprise was arriving, did ya?" Troy laughs.

"Figured it was better to let her surprise you, plus, she didn't want me to call you in case you took off." I frown down at my phone.

"What?"

"She thought we would take off with Addy if Troy gave us the heads up."

"Look, I don't get paid enough to give relationship advice. I'm just calling to let you know, Jackson's confession wasn't needed because the documentation wasn't legal or lodged so the adoption technically never happened." Troy goes on to explain that Devon will stand trial in front of a grand jury where he will be sentenced for a minimum of fifty years. Jackson will be charged and sent to prison as well. It brings me great joy to know they won't be able to sell any more children or hurt another family.

"Thanks for everything, Troy. I owe you one," Saint says.

"You owe me ten, kid, just don't ask me to cut the others out again. I work for the five of you, not just one."

"You got it, old man," Saint says before ending the call.

"We need to talk to her when she wakes up. She has to know we want her here."

"Yeah man, I agree," he answers. "Crue, what I said—"

"Don't even worry about it," I say. His eyes shine with guilt. I grip the back of his neck and pull him to me where I rest my forehead against his. "Thank you. What you did that night saved our girl and brought her home. I owe you the life of our daughter, brother."

"If you really want to thank me, you can suck my cock?" I shove him away as we both laugh.

"Been there, tried that and it's not for me, my man." He laughs harder. This right here is what I've missed. The easy banter, the way we can make each other feel okay just by being around.

"I love her, Crue."

"So do I."

"What if she wants to leave?"

"That's never going to happen," I grit out through clenched teeth.

"Good, because I don't want to live without her or Addy."

"You won't have to, we'll figure this all out. They're our girls and they stay with us always. If she has a problem with that, we'll just have to remind her why she fell in love with us. If that fails, we'll just fuck her into submission until she agrees to stay." The lustful look in Saint's eyes has my cock getting hard. I need to fuck my girl asap.

CHAPTER TWENTY

I woke up an hour ago to the sound of the guy's laughter. It brought a smile to my face hearing that sound. I decided to leave them to catch up while I snuck into my baby's room. She smiled up at me and it fucking melted my heart. I brought her back into our room and decided to run us both a bubble bath. I heard skin to skin time with a baby is the best way to bond, which is why I'm still sitting here in the bath with Addy latched onto my breast. She peed on me before and rather than be grossed out, I found it so cute. I gently brush my fingers down the side of her face and smile. I had hoped and prayed on my way back here after Troy and John got the charges dropped that she would feed from my breast.

"Hey, Momma." I dart my gaze to the doorway to see both Crue and Saint standing there, shirtless! My eyes drink them in. Jesus, it should be illegal to look that fucking good.

"Our eyes are up here, Katie baby." Humor is thick in Crue's voice. I feel the blush coating my cheeks. There's an awkwardness between us now, I hate it but I'm unsure of where the hell we stand. We had a common goal before, to find Addy. We've done that, so now what happens?

"You look lost, Momma." Hearing Saint call me Momma

shouldn't have me clenching my thighs together, but fuck it's so hot. They both step further into the room, not stopping until they reach the side of the tub, both their cocks are in line with my face. I crane my neck back to look up at them only to find their heated stares on me. "I have one question."

I swallow audibly. "What is it?" It comes out breathy and needy sounding but I can't find it within myself to care, not with how they are looking at me.

"Do you want us?" The vulnerability with which he asks robs me of air. I dart my gaze between them both and know without a doubt that I'll always want them for the rest of my life. They are the ending of my story.

"Yes." Triumphant smirks cross their faces. "But…" Their smiles falter. "I need to know if you both want this." I motion with my free hand to myself and Adalyn. "I won't give her up for you two again. If there is a choice to be made, I choose her."

Saint drops awkwardly to his knees, thanks to the moon boot, beside the tub, cups my cheek and leans in to rest his forehead against mine carefully, so he doesn't disturb Addy's feeding. "There never should have been a choice in the first place. We were so wrong and out of order to ever say the things we did. We projected our own fear of becoming like our parents onto you and that was fucking unforgivable of us to have ever done that. I know Crue has said sorry but I haven't." The sincerity in his eyes has me melting. "We left you when you needed us most. You should have been our focus, not football and getting drafted. You lost your best friend and were spiraling as well as dealing with being pregnant with our baby. We fucked up so bad, baby. I love you, Katie, and if you give us another chance to prove to you and Adalyn that we can be better, we won't let you down."

I can feel the truth in his words he means everything he has just said. If that isn't enough, the look in his eyes tells me without words how much he loves me.

"If you say no we'll just put Addy to bed and fuck a yes out of you." Saint groans and I laugh at Crue's silly comment.

"You're here now, you both showed up when our daughter needed you most and that showed me without words how much you both love her and regret your actions. I want you both always—" I don't get a chance to finish my declaration of love before Saint's mouth is on mine. He pry's my lips apart with his tongue and the moment the taste of him invades my senses, I moan.

"Dude," Crue admonishes as he yanks Saint backward until he falls on his ass. He shoots us both a glare that lacks heat. "Keep that shit PG, we don't need our girl seeing the despicable things we do to her mother."

Jesus Christ, I'm in the tub and I can already feel my pussy getting wet just from his words.

Saint, Crue and I are all lying on our bed as we watch Addy in the center, kicking her little legs and swinging her tiny arms around cooing. The three of us all have our phones out, snapping pics of our little miracle. Sitting here with them both and knowing that Saint doesn't feel any different toward Adalyn because she is biologically Crue's, has me falling in love with him all over again.

"Isn't she perfect?" Crue breathes out, in awe of our sweet girl.

"She's the most beautiful girl I've ever seen," Saint agrees.

"You got that right," I add. We spend a little longer just watching her until she begins to grow restless. I scoop her up, cradle her against me and feed her. I feel the guys' gazes boring into me. I look up to find heated lustful looks in each of their eyes.

"I never thought seeing a chick feed a baby would get me off but here I am rock-fucking-hard for my baby momma."

Saint's husky tone has me swallowing audibly and fighting the urge not to clench my thighs together.

"Ah, my bro, I feel for you." Saint and I both frown at Crue. "With how injured you are, I'm prepared to take one for the team and fuck our girl while you watch from the sideline."

Saint's eyes narrow as he glares at his best friend. "Bitch, please, you aren't coming up on my blindside with that line. I'm gonna be the one nailing her to the wall while you watch."

"Oh, fuck off, you can barely stand as it is. I really don't mind fucking her for us both and if it makes you feel better, she can scream *your* name while she comes on my cock, right, Katie baby?" I splutter when they both turn to me waiting for my answer.

Shaking my head, I decide to switch topics. "I'm gonna go put Addy to bed," I say as I unlatch her. I'm about to stand so I can burp her and take her to her crib, but Crue snakes his arms out and snatches her from me. He holds her out to Saint and me, so we can place a kiss on her head.

"Say goodnight to Mommy and Daddy, baby girl. I'll make sure Mommy doesn't scream too loud and wake you." I nearly choke on my own spit at Crue's words. Saint just chuckles and kisses our girl. We both watch Crue carrying our daughter from the room. The moment he disappears from sight, Saint grips my waist and lifts me. I squeal in surprise as he places me on his lap so I'm straddling him.

His green eyes stare up at me with nothing but love and my heart melts. "I love you, Katie."

I soften and lean down so I can clasp his face between my hands. "I love you too, always," I whisper before sealing my lips against his. His grip on my waist tightens as I deepen the kiss, then the moment I grind down against him and feel how hard he is for me already, I moan.

Breaking the kiss he stares up at me. "I need to be inside

you now, baby." The seductive way in which he delivers his demand has a shiver rolling down my spine. Without thought, I grip the hem of my shirt and yank it off, tossing it to the side. I help Saint rid himself of his own before slipping off his lap and pushing my sleep shorts down my legs. His heated gaze travels the length of my body. He bites his bottom lip and moans. "Get my cock out and fuck me, Katie baby." Not needing to be told twice, I push his pants down his legs, they stay around his knees thanks to the moon boot. My need for him is too great to worry about helping him out of that thing, I need to feel him inside me now!

Straddling his lap, I push up onto my knees and line his cock up with my opening, but before I can sink down on him, my hair is yanked and my face is pulled to the side. Crue stands there with a fistful of my hair in his grasp, his eyes burn with hunger as he stares down at me.

"Who do you belong to, Katie baby?" he growls, Heat spreads throughout my body. Crue has grown dominant and all alpha in the bedroom lately and I fucking love it.

I decide to play him at his own game. I snap my arm out, grip the back of his neck and pull him in closer until our foreheads are touching. "You and him," I answer, then mesh my lips against his. He moans into my mouth and satisfaction flows through me. Saint's grip on me tightens as he pulls me down onto his waiting cock. the second the head of his cock slips inside me, I moan wantonly, forcing Crue to break the kiss. He takes a step back and begins to undress as I ride Saint, slowly.

"Fuck, baby, you're so wet," Saint growls out approvingly as I begin to move against him. Fuck, his cock is stretching my pussy out and it feels fucking amazing. Saint reaches up and tweaks my nipples, drawing a sharp cry from me. He's careful not to squeeze my tits too hard or risk getting milk squirted on him again. Fuck, he feels so good inside me, the bed dips and I shiver in anticipation. Saint grips my hips and holds me still. I pout down at him, the bastard just smirks. "You have a choice, fuck us one at a time or—-"

I cut him off, not needing to think about my answer. "I need you both inside me at the same time, I need this." That's all it takes for Crue to push me flat against Saint's chest, then begin lubing up my ass and his cock. The moment he presses against the tight wall of muscle a moan slips past my lips. Fuck, if you've never had two cocks inside you at once, you're missing out. Crue's cock in my ass has my pussy strangling the life out of Saint's dick. The moment Crue is balls deep inside my ass, the three of us cry out, it's been a long time since I've felt this content and complete.

We fucked before but now that everything has been aired between us, and we've sorted out what needed to be sorted, the tension, hate and anger has evaporated, all that can be felt now is the love we share for each other. Crue yanks me up by my hair until my back is flush against his chest, he nuzzles the side of my neck and sucks, hard. Saint twirls my nipples between his fingers as my body begins to move on its own accord, pushing back against Crue whilst grinding down against Saint. They allow me to continue to take the lead for a minute until Crue takes charge.

Gripping the front of my throat he forces me to still. "You like both our cocks inside you, baby?" Crue's words have a moan tumbling from my lips and my pussy clamping down on Saint.

"Yeah, she does, I can feel her greedy cunt clenching my cock," Saint rasps out.

"God, please fuck me and make me come," I whimper. Crue growls as he pushes me forward so I'm flat against Saint, who captures my lips in a kiss as Crue begins to fuck my ass. Within a minute I'm moaning and screaming for them to fuck me harder. I feel their cocks growing inside me and know they are close. I feel my orgasm a second before it slams into me and rips me the fuck apart. I come screaming their names loud enough for our friends on either side of us to hear. Saint and Crue both come with my name on their lips, it gives me such sick satisfaction to know I'm the woman bringing these two Adonises to the greatest heights of pleasure.

I love that even in this fucked-up world, we are able to make our triangle of love work. Saint and Crue are everything to me and I know without a shadow of a doubt they love me with everything they have. With that knowledge, I know that in years to come we will always find a way to make our crazy, unorthodox relationship work because no matter what, our love for each other will always trump anyone and everything that tries to come between us.

EPILOGUE

Saint

One year later

We have a corporate box where we can sit and not have to worry about fans shouting to take pictures with us or being bumped around by fans, but *nooooo*, Katie had to sit in the fucking stands with everyone else so she could be closer to the field. I've taken at least fucking thirty selfies with people since the game started. Darius and Beck took great joy in offering to snap the pics for the fans. I glared at my asshole best friends, wanting to smack them across their ugly faces. The moment Katie passed Addy to me, shit changed. When a group of guys came for a pic, Darius and Beck slipped into uncle mode and told them to back the fuck up. They may give me shit but when their niece is involved, they won't allow anyone near her.

"Throw the fucking ball, Reaper!" Alexa screams from the other side of Katie.

"Fumble the ball!" Katie shouts and I fight to keep the grin off my face when Alexa pins her friend with a deadly look.

"That's my fiancée you're saying that shit too!" Lexi sneers, and Katie pins her with a scowl.

"And that's my baby daddy's team your QB is trying to beat! I told you, we weren't friends until after the game. Way to go Saints!" Katie screams right in Alexa's face. The raven-haired firecracker narrows her eyes and turns her hat around so the New England Patriots logo can be seen.

"Go the mighty fucking Patriots," Alexa screams. Val, Leah, Beck, Darius and I laugh at the crazy-ass pair. The guys and I roll our eyes. Dawson sits perched on his dad's shoulders while I hold my little one against my chest as she sleeps. Thank fuck I brought ear muffs because her mother's loud-ass mouth would have kept her up the whole game. Crue and Corvin's teams are playing each other tonight. We made a deal that no matter what, whenever our teams would play each other, we would all be there. I have to fly out tonight to make it back for my game tomorrow.

This past year has been fucking incredible. Katie and Addy stay at our house in CHU for now until she finishes college, but Crue or me always try to get back to them as often as we can. She flies to us sometimes but we don't like her traveling alone with Addy. It's crazy as fuck to juggle everything but with the help of my brothers and the girls, we make it work.

Everything I have ever wanted is finally happening, I got the girl *and* I even got my guy. I fucking love Crue, he's my brother, best friend and… he's my future brother husband, as we call it. We've never fucked or done anything since that day over a year ago, but we don't need to because Katie is the reason why we are able to love each other freely without acting on it.

"Baby, tell her she is out of her fucking mind!" I shake my head and look at my girl frowning. She has an angry look on her face and I tense. Katie has a bad fucking temper and Crue and I do anything we can to not get on the bad side of her because normally our dicks pay the price, and let me tell you, getting a six-inch heel to your cock is not fucking fun!

"Baby, whatever it is, I'm sorry and I won't do it again," I plead. Darius and Beck laugh while Katie frowns.

"What?' she asks, confused.

"What?" I say, trying to keep her confused so she doesn't remember why she's mad.

"Just tell Alexa that Crue is hotter than Corvin." I snort and meet Alexa's gaze over Katie's head.

"Sorry, *Lex Luther*, Crue wins hands down every time." Alexa growls and rolls her eyes.

"His vote doesn't count! He sleeps with him as well so he's biased." I snicker but keep quiet at Alexa's outburst. She turns to Leah and Val. "Tell her that Corvin is better looking." Leah cringes in disgust and Val shakes her head.

"Nope. I vote for Beckett and that's final," Val says in a matter-of-fact tone.

"Damn good fucking answer, baby," Beck says from my other side.

Leah smiles sheepishly and Alexa gasps. "You bitch," Lexi seethes.

"He's my brother and he's... eww." D, Beck and I all laugh at Leah's answer.

I tune out the girls bickering and just soak in this moment with my family, I never thought we would ever get here. I always thought I would never find a way out from under Devon's thumb, but with the help of my brothers I was able to buy my freedom until the cunt decided to go after my daughter. He crossed a line and now he will spend the rest of his days in a supermax prison, hopefully getting his ass fucked raw daily.

"Daddy." The sound of my daughter's melodic voice pulls me from my wayward thoughts. I lift her up and cuddle her against me. Adalyn has become my sole reason for pushing to achieve everything I set out to do, so I can show my daughter that the sky's the limit for her and she can be whatever she wants. I'll never dull or try to diminish her dreams like my father did to me. I'll make sure that I am her number one fan and always there to support her, no matter what. "You caprice, Mommy?" My eyes widen and I shoot a look at Katie to make sure she isn't paying attention to us.

I shift the ear muff off one of her ears and whisper, "Not yet, princess. We have to wait for Daddy to finish playing before we ask Mommy." Crue and I plan to ask Katie to marry us tonight, it's not legal in the US but we found that we can have a handfasting ceremony done in Budapest where our marriage will be legal there and Katie will finally no longer be Katie Turner, she will be known as Katie Hastings-Morgan. I can't wait to blindside her with our question.

EPILOGUE

The next year

"Why the fuck do we have to do this?" Saint whines from beside me. Rolling my eyes, I lull my head to the side and pin him with a bored look.

"Because our wife told us to sit our asses here, so shut the fuck up before I don't get laid tonight because of your bitching." Saint glares at me and huffs out his annoyance as he crosses his arms over his chest and pouts. Darius sits on Saint's other side while Beck and Corv sit next to me, all currently seated in front of a runway. Apparently this is Nathan's first big show. The guy is some high-end fashion designer for women's lingerie and truthfully, I think he will be good at it. It took Saint a minute to come around to forgiving him for signing over our rights to Addy, but after Nate explained why and apologized Saint eventually forgave him.

"When the hell does this shit start?" Corvin grumbles from beside me. Much like Saint and me, he just flew into town tonight and the three of us have been away for nearly six weeks at boot camp and just want to fuck our girls all night long.

"Chill the fuck out, it'll start soon," Darius quips from the other end of our row. We haven't even been able to see our daughter. She's out back with her mother and the other girls. Our thoughts are muted the moment Nathan comes out on the stage and the crowd erupts into cheers and catcalls.

"Thank you all so much for being here tonight. I am beyond grateful for all the support I received over the years and honestly, I wouldn't have been able to do any of this without the support of my crew." The moment his gaze strays to us in the front seats at the end of the runway we all tense in our seats. "Thank you to my CHU boys for always accepting me for who I am and welcoming me with nothing but love." The crowd all cheers and I'll admit, I'm humbled by his words. "I also have to give a shout to my bad bitches, Katie Hastings-Morgan, Leah Williams, Valance Dawson and Alexa Williams." Corvin cheers loudly at hearing his wife's name, the fucker is such a caveman since he married her a couple months ago. "Without these girls, I wouldn't be here. So, with all that said, I would like to dedicate this show to my OG bad bitch Cody Sutton." All of us gasp. "This one is for you, baby girl."

None of us say a word as Nathan exits the stage, we had no idea this show was a dedication to Cody. Jeremih ft YG's "Don't Tell 'Em" begins to play and the lights dim. The curtains at the end of the stage part and the moment the girl comes into view my jaw unhinges. Alexa struts toward us in a white lace getup with garters and all, her long black hair is out and flowing behind her, she even has black angel wings on. Her blue eyes are glued to her husband who is sitting there openmouthed with his eyes wide in shock. The moment she stops at the end of the catwalk, she strikes a pose and blows her man a kiss. When she turns and we all get a view of her ass in a thong, Corvin finally snaps out of it.

"Close your fucking eyes assholes!" he shouts. We all laugh and tease him until Beckett stills beside me, his eyes wide as fuck.

"The fuck!" Beck snaps as the song changes to TLC's "No Scrubs". I turn back to see Val walking toward us in an outfit similar to Lexi's but red and her wings are the same color as her sexy outfit. Beck attempts to stand but Corv and I hold him in place as Val strikes her pose and winks at her man before turning around and making her way back. Before he can say the words, we all slam our eyes shut. It's taking everything inside me not to laugh at my boy's expense. The moment the song switches to Ella Mai's, "Whatchamacallit", Darius is on his feet and the four of us are holding him back as Leah appears at the end of the stage. She wears a one-piece yellow lacey getup. Her tits are pushed up and her nipples are barely covered. The long angel wings flow behind her, and her blonde hair is done in some fancy updo.

"Goldie!" Darius roars as he fights against us. Leah, being the little temptress she is, winks and smiles at her man. She strikes her pose and makes sure to hold his gaze the entire time until she is forced to turn away. "I'm gonna fucking chain her ass up," Darius seethes.

Chris Brown's "Under The Influence" begins to play, then Saint and I are both gawking at the stage entrance with bated breath. Sure enough, our queen comes strutting out with a fierce look on her face. The white bralette thing she wears makes her tits look huge and the panties, OMG, they barely cover her beautiful pussy. Her gaze is on us the whole way but the closer she gets to the end, I see nervousness cloud her features. I begin to worry something is wrong so I mouth, *you got this, baby.*

A small smile pulls at her lips as she stops to strike her pose but unlike the other girls, Katie turns side on and rubs both her hands over her stomach and smiles nervously. That's when I notice the tiny bump. Saint and I both gasp in unison.

As if our minds are in sync we both dart forward and leap onto the stage, not giving a fuck about the fashion show as we stand in front of our wife who has tears in her eyes. Saint cups her face between his hands and bends so he is eyes level with her.

"We're having a baby?" Shock is evident in his voice as she bites her lip and nods.

"We need the words, baby," I growl. She darts her gaze to me and the fear I see in her gaze kills me. We are the reason she is so fucking terrified to tell us she's pregnant but this time it will be different.

"Yes." No sooner has the word left her mouth when Saint's lips plaster against hers. I give him a minute before I'm shoving him out of the way and kissing my girl, making sure she can feel all the love I have for her. I break the kiss and drop to my knees in front of her placing a kiss against her tiny bump.

"I love you already, my little bean." A sob comes from my girl before Saint is kissing her again. Nathan shouts for us to get the hell off the stage, and with pleasure I obey and we drag our girl off the stage, hunting around for the nearest dressing room so I can show her with my cock just how happy I am about this news.

We're about to be a family of five and I'm fucking here for it!

EPILOGUE

Corvin

A year after Nathan's show

At twenty-four years old I never thought I would be the type of guy who longed to be able to be home alone with a wife just so I could have her all to myself. I thought at this age I would be partying it up with my brothers and living out my dream of playing for the NFL and being the most eligible bachelor out there, but nope, instead here I am with my wife at our house in CHU with our two nephews and niece while their parents are out on a date night.

Dawson is easy as fuck, he's eight and can do shit for himself, but Addy is only three and Alister is six months old, so he needs constant attention. Sitting next to her on the sofa, a smile tugs at my lips at the sight of my badass wife feeding our nephew a bottle and talking quietly to him. I get so lost in thoughts of her one day sitting there, doing that with our own child that I don't see the dirty diaper she throws at my head until it smacks me in the forehead.

"What the fuck, jail bait?" I growl. The dirty little minx smirks and shrugs her shoulders.

"Didn't your mother ever tell you it's rude to stare?" she quips.

Narrowing my eyes I snap back, "That ring on your finger says I can do whatever the fuck I like where you are concerned, woman." Her brows raise to her hairline.

"Woman?" Oh fuck, I gulp and smile sheepishly. I love my wife with every fiber of my being but I am man enough to fucking admit she terrifies me! That woman can hold a grudge like no other. She is not above prank wars or breaking my shit if I piss her off.

"I meant it in a funny way, you know like *me Tarzan you Jane?"* Her face turns stoic and I begin to panic, I know that look and it normally means Mrs. Palmer is going to be getting a workout for the next four days until she eventually forgives me, only because she's just as fucking horny as I am.

"I should key your car." I groan and send a silent prayer to God that she doesn't. She owns a shop in New England and one here in CHU. The girl is a master mechanic and builds an engine from scratch. My girl isn't afraid to get dirty and honestly, it's fucking hot to see her in her shop ordering the guys who work for her around. Just the thought gets my dick hard.

"Please don't," I beg. A smug smile tugs at her lips. The last time she did that I told her to fix it and even got my man voice on and everything. When I flew back into town and saw a hot pink MC20 Cielo Spyder pull up to the curb at the pickup zone at the airport, my jaw was on the ground. She painted my car fucking pink to teach me a lesson for yelling at her. She stands and carefully places Alister in his portable crib before coming over to me and straddling my lap. I'm stiff as a fucking tree trunk waiting for her to strike out and maim me or something, but when her eyes soften I frown. "What's wrong?"

"Do you love me, Reaper?" I search her gaze for a second, slightly worried that something is seriously wrong. Cupping her face between my hands, I pull her down to me until my lips ghost over hers.

"More than anything in this fucking world, baby," I say with such conviction, there is no way she can deny my words.

"Do you love me enough to wait until I'm ready to have a baby?" Her question has me frowning and wondering where the fuck that shit came from but before I can ask she pushes on, "I see you watching me with the kids. Don't get me wrong, I fucking love them and enjoy being around them, but I'm not ready to be a mom and honestly—" She takes a deep breath before continuing, "I'm not ready to share you with anyone yet. I love us just the way we are."

My heart beats double time in my chest. Alexa isn't the type of girl who will tell you how she feels, she'll show you with actions and honest to God, I fucking love that about her. I know her using her words was fucking hard, it makes me so proud of her every time I see her trying to use her words instead of breaking shit. Some may think it's toxic but honestly, that's just us. We fight hard but let me assure you we love fucking harder. This girl would go to war for me, she proved that when my coach tried to bench me for missing a practice. She marched her little ass into his office and screamed and hollered until he changed his mind. The poor guy just clapped me on the shoulder and told me I was a brave man for putting a ring on that woman.

"Baby, I don't need a kid to be happy." Relief shines in her eyes at my words. "I love us just the way we are and I sure as fuck love that I get to fuck you anytime and anywhere I want. Having a kid will put a damper on that, and I'm not down for that shit." She laughs and I smile loving hearing the sound of her laughter. "We have all the time in the world for that, jail bait. Let's just enjoy us for us for now and when the time does come, we'll deal with it then."

She smashes her mouth to mine and within a second, I'm rock hard beneath her. She grinds down against me, drawing a groan of approval from me. I grip her waist and force her down onto me so I can—

"Eww." I practically throw her off me and jump to my feet as I face Dawson, who stands in the doorway with a disgusted look on his face. Alexa is too busy laughing her ass off to worry that we could have scared the shit out of our nephew. I turn and glare down at her.

"We are so not having kids for at least ten years." We both break out into uncontrollable laughter at my words. I fucking love my life and my wife, she is my Hail Mary pass I never fumbled.

EPILOGUE

A year later

Christmas used to be a time of year I didn't much care for but now, I look forward to it each year because it means we all come together as a family at our cabin. No matter what life throws at us, we always make it to the cabin every single year without fail and celebrate Christmas and the New Year together. Now that we have Dawson, Adalyn and Alister, Christmas is just that much more special because we get to wake up and see the wonder on their faces when they see all the gifts beneath the tree.

"When?" I snap my gaze to the side to see Leah and Darius standing there, the angry look in Leah's eyes tells me she is pissed.

"Why do you have to have a ring? I tell you every fucking day I love you, what the hell does a ring mean compared to the words?" She throws her hands up in the air in frustration, Darius still hasn't popped the question and Leah is getting tired of waiting for him to man up and ask her to marry him.

"Don't you want to be with me... forever?" The water tone of her voice tells me she is close to tears. I take a step forward out of the kitchen only for a hand to grip my arm. I turn to see my own wife standing there with a stern look on her face.

"You can't fix this one for her," she says quietly. My shoulders droop, knowing she's right but still wanting to be there for her. Leah is one of my best friends and I'm so grateful my wife understands that is all that is between us and nothing more.

"He's an idiot," I mumble. Val smiles lovingly up at me.

"He is," she says with an eye roll and I chuckle. "But, it's still his relationship, not yours. You need to let them sort this one out, big man." I nod my agreement. I know she's right, it's just hard to watch Leah every year wait for Darius to finally pop the question only for the New Year to roll around and still have no ring. A sob coming from Leah draws my attention as she races toward the stairs. Val sighs and pats me on the chest. "I'll go check on her," she says, but before she can move past me, I snap my arm out and grip the back of her neck, yanking her back to me.

"Where the fuck do you think you're going, Valance?" I growl as a shiver works its way through her body at my words. She peers up at me through her long lashes, her breaths coming in short rapid pants.

"I-I was just..." My lips are on hers cutting off her rambling. Even after all these years my hunger for her never lessens. Val is my everything, my soulmate in every sense of the word. I would be nothing without her, which is why every morning I leave for work, I make sure to tell her how much I love her and show it with my actions. Like getting up two hours earlier than her to clean the house, sort everything for Dawson for the day and get him up and ready for school, so all she has to do is worry about getting herself set for the day.

Breaking the kiss, I rest my forehead against hers and stare into her eyes as I say, "I love you, Val, more than anything.

You will always be it for me, in this life and the next. It's always been you for me." Tears cloud her eyes as she stares up at me.

"I love you too, more than you will ever know, big man. I'm always gonna be here, till death do us part, remember?" I smile, loving the sound of that. As I release her and slap her ass, she sashays away. Every day she reminds me we're forever and endgame no matter what.

"How the fuck do you do it?" I turn to see Darius leaning against the breakfast counter looking annoyed.

"Do what?"

"That," he says, motioning toward Val's retreating frame.

"Easy," I say with a shrug. "I love her and would do anything to make her happy. No matter how scared it makes me, I would do it because I would know that at the end of the day it would bring a smile to her face."

He scoffs and rolls his eyes. "Dude, I bought Leah her dream house on the beach. She wanted to dance again so I go to all her shows and cheer her on. I come home every night and I'm there every morning she wakes up. What the fuck more does she want?" I can hear the frustration in his tone and I want to slap him, he's a fucking idiot.

"Darius, she loves you and always has since she was like fourteen. You are the happy ending she has always wanted. If you two don't work out, she will base all her future relationships on *you*. Every guy that comes into her life and loves her, she will base on *you*. You are the example she will use for the rest of her life. She will compare every person she loves to you because she will never love anyone as much as she loves you. If you meet someone else and have a daughter, you will never see her face in that child no matter how much you wish you could. Can you live the rest of your life without her? Can you risk her growing tired of waiting for you to finally make her Leah Lockhart?"

His eyes darken as he stares at me with an angry glint in

his eyes. "I'll kill any cunt who tries to take her from me. Leah is mine!" he snarls. I smirk and cross my arms over my chest.

"Hm, maybe you might want to go put a ring on that shit then, before she finds herself a new *halfback*."

"Go fuck yourself, *Becky*," he snaps.

"Nah, man, my *wife* fucks beautifully every single night after we put our son to bed. My cock is taken care of so don't you worry. Can you say the same about yours though?" His eyes narrow to slits.

"What Val sees in you I'll never know," he grumbles just as Val enters the kitchen again.

"I see my happiness. I see my world, I see the love of my life and my Endgame." Fuck yeah. I don't use words, instead I grab my wife and fling her over my shoulder caveman-style and head for the stairs, because we are out of earshot, I call back to Darius.

"Be a good uncle and watch your nephew while I go make him a sister."

EPILOGUE

Darius

That same Christmas

I watch her as everyone opens their gifts and she waits for me to finally man up and ask the question she has been dying for me to ask for the past four years. I fight the smirk from breaking free when all the presents are opened and still, she has no ring. She drops her gaze to her lap and tries to fight the sadness from overshadowing her day with the family. Corvin proposed to Alexa on Christmas and I refuse to take a leaf out of his book. I never do things the way people expect me to which is why, I'm not proposing to her today.

She stays in a sour mood for the rest of the day. Beck is shooting me daggers every chance he gets, but I ignore it. Saint and Crue are too wrapped up in chasing their demonic kids around. Honest to God, Karma got them good because Adalyn is so much like Saint while Alister is like Crue and fuck, it's hilarious watching them both fight with kids daily. Corvin chooses to turn a blind eye to anything with me and his sister, it's better that way so it doesn't come between us and our friendship.

For the next six days Leah barely speaks to me. She won't

even angry fuck, and now I'm starting to get fucking pissed off because the girl is icing me out. I'm not down with not being able to sink my cock into her every night. Being inside her pussy is my happy place, and the fact she is denying me is going to make my revenge so much sweeter when she realizes she has been a fucking brat. She'll be on her knees three times a day sucking up to me. Yes, I said sucking because that is the only way she is going to make this up to me.

"Corv, I need a word." At the serious tone of my voice, he doesn't fuck around. He gets off the sofa and follows me outside onto the deck. I shiver from the cold but I have to do this, I can't go behind his back.

"Dude, it's freezing, what's up?" I stare at my best friend and hope to God he doesn't give me a black eye.

"I love your sister."

He frowns. "I know."

Shaking my head, I push on. "No, I mean I love her so fucking much, and honestly, I know at the start I played offside with some of the dumb shit I did, but I can't live without her."

Corvin looks worried. "What the fuck is going on, Darius?"

Sucking a deep breath, I decide to just come out with it. "I want your blessing to ask Leah to marry me. I love you, brother, but even if you say no, I'm going to marry her anyway because I fucking love her, Corv. She is mine and I won't ever let her go—"

He cuts me off by placing a hand on my shoulder and smiling wide. "I've been waiting for you to man up and make an honest woman out of her. I'd love nothing more than to see my sister happy and I know you are the reason why she smiles so much. I love my sister, D. I also know you love her way more than I ever could. You have my blessing, brother, always."

It's close to ten by the time Crue and Saint get their kids to bed. They both look fucking wrecked and I can't help but laugh at them when they walk into the living room. "Go fuck yourself, asshole," Saint quips out.

"Let's not, I don't want to know what my sister does," Corvin chimes in from his place at the counter.

"Well, your sister isn't doing him," Leah grits out from her place next to Beck on the sofa across from me.

"Oh snap," Crue gleefully says as he drops down beside me and flings his arm around my shoulders. I smack the fucker away and pin him with a glare.

"Don't be mad at him because you're a jackass." Oh fuck this, I'm on my feet in a second glaring down at my girlfriend. Crue, Saint, Beck and even Corvin stand and creep toward me. I roll my eyes as I look at each of them.

"Let's get shit clear here, okay?" I say to the guys. "Crowd around me all you like but I'm never going to lay a hand on her no matter how fucking crazy she makes me. The only place I will beat her is in her pants, and lets be real, Corv, your sister loves it when I beat that pussy up." Corvin rushes me but Beck intervenes and holds him back. Leah stands and pushes into me.

"You are a real prick—"

"And you fucking love it, Goldie. Now shut up and listen." She clamps her mouth closed. I hear Alexa, Val and Katie gasp from behind me but I ignore them. "You are such an impatient brat. You drive me fucking crazy and make me question my sanity daily." Her face falls and fear begins to fill her eyes thinking I'm about to break up with her. "But, I wouldn't have it any other way because I love your crazy ass.

You were made for me, Goldie. We all get one chance at finding our perfect match in life, and your psychotic ass is mine." Tears trail down her cheeks. I gently cup her face between my hands and stare into her eyes. "I'm sorry for ever making you doubt what you mean to me. I love you with everything that I am. I'm nothing without you, Leah. You are the only girl I have ever kissed, you're the first girl I have ever loved and risked everything for. There is no way in hell I would ever let you go, even if you wanted to. I had planned to do this at midnight, but you had to go and be all dramatic and piss me off."

She chuckles but I see the nervousness in her eyes. I place a quick kiss to her lips as I step back, grip the box from my back pocket and lower to one knee. Her hands come up to cover her mouth as tears flow freely down her cheeks, peering down at me. I open the box to show her the black diamond ring on a white gold band that is encrusted with little diamonds.

"Leah Williams, I have loved you since I was sixteen years old. You were my first crush, my first and only love. You make me a better man and I want to spend the rest of my life with you. Fuck, Goldie, just say yes and marry me so I can finally call you *Leah Lockhart*."

"I love you too," she cries out as she drops to her knees in front of me, wraps her arms around my neck and meshes her lips to mine. I deepen the kiss without thought and fucking love the way she melts into me, then it clicks in my mind.

Pulling back I break the kiss and ask, "So, is that a yes?"

She smiles. "Fuck yes, you scored the touchdown, halfback."

Thank you!

HOLY FUCKING SHITBALLS...

I have debated so many times on how to end this book and I thought what better way than an extended epi from each of the guys.
Thank you so much for reading Blindside. I loved Crue and Saint from the start, but I was never sure if they would ever get a book and I am so fucking glad they got one because fuck me, they deserved it.
How freaking cute were Saint and Crue when they finally got over themselves and fell in love with their daughter and Katie?
I can't say it enough, but from the bottom of my heart thank you for reading, Offside, Touchdown, Endgame, Hail Mary and Blindside.
If you would be so kind as to leave a review on Amazon, Bookbub and/or Goodreads that would be amazing.

Also by Samantha Barrett

PARANORMAL ROMANCE

The Dream Series

The Dream Trilogy

A Beautiful Dream

A Twisted Fate

A Beautiful Nightmare

Redemption

Anarchy

Brutal Savages

Savage Lies

Brutal Truth

Savage Beast

Brutal Beauty

MAFIA ROMANCE

Murdoch Mafia Series

Played By The Bishop

Tormented By The King

Tortured By The Knight

Tempted By The Queen

Turned By The Pawn

Ruined By The Rook

<u>Fairytales With A Twist</u>

Condemned Beast

SPORTS ROMANCE

<u>Playing For Keeps</u>

<u>Duet</u>

Offside

Touchdown

End Game

Hail Mary

Blindside

RH SPORTS

Hate Us Like You Mean It

Acknowledgments

Baby daddy, what can I say… Well there is so much I can say but I also love being married to you, so I will just say thank you for allowing me to use you as my MM dummy and allowing me to try things out on you–I kid, he never let me do shit much to my dismay. Love you, big daddy D.

My babies, my reason for existing. I love you both more than you will ever know. Without the both of you I am nothing. You give me purpose every day just by being you and loving me the way you do. You both are the best story I have and will ever write.

My Alpha girls, Clare, Sarah and Tash. Holy shit, from the Mafia to Beast, than to Hate Us and Now we have a complete series, ladies. None of these books would be where they are or what they are without each of you. Thank you so fucking much for believing in me and pushing me.

My Army: Alicia, Amber, Angel, Ash, Barb, Charlotte, Cyndi, Christina, Debbie, Jasmine, Jen, Kahanna, Katelyn, Kylie, Lakshmi, Lora, Lyndsey, Rebecca, Rizzo, Sarmi, Sonya, Terri and Tess. Thank you ladies so fucking much for being the best freaking team an author could ask for. I owe you all so much for the love and dedication you give me. None of these books would be where they are without you all hyping them up and loving each of these guys as much as I do.

My street team and Christina motherfucking Santos. Thank you so much for everything you do and all the shares as well as pimping out each of these books all over the socials, you ladies are amazing!

Natasha Joanne, my love. I adore and can't thank you enough for all you do. Got to be honest, so glad you are forcing me to take a break because this one killed me—5 days, 5 fucking days to write a book. Man I'm dead lol.

My editor, Lizz. Fucking hell, you are amazing! Thank you so much for continuing to love each of my books and making them all pretty for me. You truly are a star, my friend.

Leah Maree, my love as per usual you smashed this fucking cover out of the park. You are so beyond talented and I am in awe of you. Thank you for making these covers so epic for the whole series, because it was all you, boo, and your crazy ass brain.

Sarah Wilson, I have to give you a special shout out, babe, because of you being honest and being straight with me, I rewrote this book and I am so fucking glad. You made me strive for perfection while writing this one and honestly, I am beyond blessed to call you my friend. Xx

Clare Bear, I love you. I know this has been a trying time for you with everything you are going through, but the fact you still read these books for me means more than you will ever know. I love you.

Last but not least, you, my amazing readers, mean everything to me! Without you, none of this would be possible. Thank you for your continued support and reading my books. It still stuns me to get messages from you telling me you love my books. I really am living my dream and that's thanks to you.

Sam

About the Author

Samantha Barrett is a dark romance, PNR author who loves to write out-of-the-box stories. She is originally from the land of the long white cloud, New Zealand. She is totally fluking her way through this whole author gig, if she isn't writing you can find her kicking back with her kids and husband with a bag of chips and a glass of wine in her hand.
Sam loves Twilight and is a TWIHARD proudly.

www.ingramcontent.com/pod-product-compliance
Lightning Source LLC
Chambersburg PA
CBHW060600190726
48283CB00003B/1097